The Jade Dragon

Wyvern Chronicles

Nix Whittaker

Shilong gazed at the airships in the airport. They were clustered close enough together that someone daring enough could hop from one ship to another. The airships bobbed in the gentle breeze blowing in from the coast. They stayed stationary because they were connected to thick ropes that were looped through holes bored into large stones on the ground.

The port made an alleyway with businesses on one side and the moored ships on the other. The businesses catered to the ships that harboured here to restock after a long trip over the sea.

The airships were mostly wide, flat-bottomed hulls, which made it easy to carry cargo. Shilong scanned the ships for one in particular—one that his contact said carried a dragon.

He tucked his hands into the pockets of his western-style pants as he sauntered among the people who worked the port. People walked briskly about their business. Women leaned close to each other while men walked as if they had to be somewhere in a hurry. The clothes were a mixture of western-style suits and dresses from the Wyvern Empire, and the local, more elaborate kimonos and wooden shoes, a homage to the local culture.

The Nipponese traded with the rest of the world, while Han had been an isolated country for centuries, refusing to trade with the outside world. Shilong was only a visitor to Nippon, though his own country of Han wasn't far as the dragon flew.

Fitting into the crowd was easy, as he had the same straight black hair as the local Nipponese people. Taller than the average man in the multitude, he wasn't tall enough to stand out. His appearance did make it possible for him to stroll through the masses and to study the airships without being noticed by the foreigners. Anyone from Nippon who saw him would recognize the touches that said he came from the mainland, so he didn't want to be obvious in his search.

Shilong found the ship he was looking for and paused to admire the Blazing Blunderbuss. It was a sleek ship and the weapons on it were as elegant as its body. Clearly the ship could handle pirates. He had heard there was a dragon on board the Blazing Blunderbuss who had mated to a human woman. Very curious, as dragons didn't like to surround themselves with humans.

A woman stood by the side of the lift watching the dock workers load the supplies. Shilong hesitated to study her for a moment. She was wearing a prim dress that was practical rather than stylish, and her hair was equally prim and practical as it was set in a single braid pinned up in a few loops. The braid was long and a deep chestnut brown. Stunned by the sudden craving to untie the woman's hair to see how long it would be, Shilong took his hands out of his pockets before he even realised. He had been suppressing his own urges for so long he was almost astonished he could still feel something for an interesting woman.

He pushed the impulse away. With a mission to complete, Shilong knew it would not do to be distracted. With that thought firmly in his mind he progressed towards the Blazing Blunderbuss and the woman manning the lift.

Glancing at him as he approached, she didn't appear nervous. Either she was confident that she could handle him or she was naïve. He nodded in greeting to her.

"I am Shilong, and I require a berth on your ship to travel to Han," he said in perfect Imperial, which was a mixture of all the languages that made up the Wyvern Empire.

The woman looked him over. "Can you pay?"

He pulled out some coins. They were round with a square cut out of the middle and threaded on a string to make them easier to carry. He tugged on a knot and dropped the whole string of coins into her hand.

"When do you need to go?" she asked as she counted.

"Today."

She smiled, transforming her face to something transcendent. Their hands brushed lightly as he took back the coins she offered.

"Excellent, we're going that way and we've just finished loading the cargo. I'm the first mate, Alice."

She indicated for him to jump on the lift. There wasn't much space on the platform so Shilong stepped up close to her. At least that's what he told himself. She flipped the lever and they started to rise to the ship above.

He still couldn't figure out if it was confidence or naïvety as he took in her scent. She smelled of roses and wood polish. He wasn't used to human women who didn't simper in fear at his presence. If they knew who he was they usually just screamed and ran.

A young man waited on the deck for them and grinned at Alice as the lift came to a stop. For that small gesture of warm greeting, Shilong wanted to tear him up.

Shilong took another look at the woman. She had introduced herself as the first mate of this airship and he put his feelings aside for now. He was here for a reason and his loyalties would be divided if he decided to pursue his desires.

His contacts in Nippon had been vague on what they had discovered about the Blazing Blunderbuss. Mainly they had told him outrageous stories: how it had once been a pirate ship until a dragon had stolen it. He wondered where the dragon was. Maybe he could complete his mission quickly and leave before he was compromised by his urge to collect the woman that was the first mate.

"I'll give you a tour while Liam deals with our supplies." Alice waved to indicate the young man.

"You aren't going to introduce the new passenger?" Liam asked with a raised eyebrow.

"Fine. Shilong, this is Liam, our engineer." Shilong looked at the young man with some surprise. His contacts had told him the engineer was a woman and she was descended from a line of great tinkers. This young man clearly wasn't the same person he had heard about. He wondered what other information had been inaccurate.

Shilong flicked a look at the first mate to see if she had any of the mating marks a person would have if they were bonded to a dragon. She was free of any marks so she was unlikely to be the dragon's mate.

The young man offered his hand and Shilong took a long moment to realise it was the greeting Westerners used. He also become conscious Alice had not tried to shake his hand before.

Alice said gently, "They don't shake hands here, Liam. Just pack everything away. You'll have a chance to speak to our guest later. He's travelling with us until Han."

Liam dropped his hand and shrugged.

Following after Alice, Shilong said, "I hope I didn't give any offence."

"Not in the least. Liam is young. He doesn't realise there are different customs in different places. We've been travelling through the East for weeks now, but he's mostly been working in smithies instead of dealing with merchants who are very proper in the way things need to be done."

"Who taught you to deal with the Akinai?" Shilong asked, impressed with her grasp of the local culture.

"I read," Alice said defensively. They travelled further into the ship. "This is the mess hall. Most will be gathered in here as it's almost time for our midday meal. We'll stop here first and I'll show you your cabin after the meal."

Accepting this, he nodded and followed her into the narrow room. There a woman cooking, but she was not a homey type typical of a ship's cook. She wore breeches and had short hair. Alice greeted the woman and turned to Shilong for the introductions. "This is Susan. She's our cook and she's Murphy's lady."

Susan, without turning from the pan she was cooking from, said, "Hey, I'm more than somebody's lady, and besides, we're just friends."

Alice rolled her eyes. "You're a friend who shares his room and if I'm not mistaken you're not interested in being anyone else's friend. In any case we don't want a repeat of what happened with the last passenger."

The cook winced. "Yeah, I suppose, but why do you have to introduce me that way, as if I'm defined by who I'm shacked up with?"

Alice waved towards Shilong. "It's for our guest. He's male and mightn't realise the complexities of female identity."

Chuckling, Susan glanced in Shilong's direction. "You should be offended, mate. She just insulted you."

Shilong shook his head. "I understand why she stated that you're someone who has a particular friend. It is to stop misunderstandings later." He knew he was too deep when he asked without thinking, "May I ask, first mate, do you have a particular friend?"

Laughing quietly at the question, Susan turned back to her cooking and left Alice to answer. Alice's cheeks turned pink. "No one in particular. Not that it's any of your business."

Shilong was about to offer an opportunity for her to be his particular friend when a man entered the room. He shooed away a metal dragon that was the size of a large bird. "Ow, get off me, you hunk of sacrilegious metal."

Flapping her flipper in the direction of the newcomers, Susan said, "I told you she would notice if you used one of her nuts."

"I needed it. The bolt was loose on my Lucy." He patted a weapon on his hip. The small mechanical dragon screeched, making everyone in the room wince. The man sighed. "Fine, you beast. You can have it back."

Pulling the weapon off his hip, he unscrewed a small nut and passed it to the miniature dragon. The dragon chittered and went to a small bowl sitting on the table and carefully placed the nut inside.

Alice gestured to the man with the gun. "This is Murphy, our gunner."

Murphy indubitably had enough weapons on him for a gunner—astonishing, as they were not in any danger at that moment. Considering Murphy had given names to his weapons, Shilong had to assume the man habitually carried weapons.

Shilong wasn't here for him because Murphy wasn't the most dangerous person on this ship. Shilong had been sent to make sure the Wyvern Empire dragon did not cause any trouble. Shilong had not yet come across the dragon or his mate, the tinker.

———————

Alice eyed the new passenger. He was either a local or from the region at large as he had the straight black hair common to the Nipponese people. His eyes were narrow and a stunning green colour. Almost like jade. He held himself so still, unlike Liam or Murphy who seemed to talk mostly with their arms. The stillness fascinated her.

Shilong watched her with his green, green eyes. She blushed when she realised he had caught her staring and she flicked away her gaze.

Murphy asked, "Do you think Hara will be here for lunch?"

"Unlikely. She usually has morning sickness about this time of the day," Susan said casually.

Murphy asked, "Morning sickness? I thought you only got that in the morning." He wasn't completely shocked Hara was pregnant, but then Hara and Gideon had been going at it like bunnies for the last three months. Alice, on the other hand, felt like someone had taken a wrench to the side of her head.

Getting over her astonishment that she hadn't noticed the symptoms in her captain, Alice answered Murphy. "No, morning sickness can strike at any time of the day, though usually at the same time each day and only in the first few months." She wished Hermia, their on-board doctor, was in the mess to answer these questions. Hermia was resting as she had been working day and night with a local physician.

Susan snorted. "Unless you're bloody unlucky and have morning sickness to the day you pop."

Alice winced at the description. About to make a comment, she hesitated when she heard someone at the door. Hara and Gideon entered the mess.

Hara bowed her head in greeting and sat down. She looked pale and Alice wondered if she should place a bowl next to her.

Gideon distracted Alice by the way he looked at Shilong. He almost glared, and Gideon never glared.

Finally, Gideon asked, "Are you here to cause trouble?" Gideon didn't usually pay attention to any passengers as he considered them Hara's responsibility.

A strange question for a harmless passenger, but Shilong bowed his head respectfully to the question. "I am here to prevent trouble."

Gideon narrowed his eyes. "You keep it that way."

Alice had never seen Gideon go so cold on someone without even knowing them. He was so gregarious she would have expected a joke rather than this cautious awareness. She had heard stories that one time when he had been kidnapped, he had suggested his kidnappers join him in adventurous sex involving silk rope.

Alice would ask Gideon later what that was all about, because right then things were getting interesting as

Murphy asked Hara, "Can you really get morning sickness any time of the day, Hara?"

Hara frowned. She must be very ill, as normally she was as sharp as one of Murphy's blades. Alice shifted closer to the bowls and was about to fish one out when Hara asked, "Why are you asking me?"

Susan said, "'Cos you have morning sickness, or didn't you know?"

Hara waved her hand lethargically. "Impossible. Well, not impossible, but certainly unlikely. Gideon is a dragon and I'm human."

Centuries earlier, dragons had come to earth. Most people hadn't noticed the invasion because they could take on the shape of humans. It wasn't until the dragons had decided to try take over the world that things had changed dramatically. No one knew who first thought of sending off people as tributes to the dragons, but it was a common practice for years. It might have stayed the status quo except one of the women collected by the dragons became pregnant. The dragons no longer hunted humans, and instead sorted them out as mates.

"We can't be too compatible..." Her voice drifted off at the end of the sentence as her confidence disappeared. She looked up at Gideon, who hadn't taken a seat yet. "Right?"

Gideon shifted his eyes from Shilong to Hara. "You are most likely pregnant." Gideon liked his certainties as he was a professor of mathematics. It was unusual for him to prevaricate.

Hara yelped, "What?" She jumped to her feet in shock, but that only made her quickly put a hand to her mouth. She shook her head and pushed away from the table. Alice passed her a bowl and Hara gave her a look of thanks before she grabbed the bowl and dashed out of the room.

Gideon took a seat and Alice asked, "Aren't you going after her?"

Gideon snorted at what he clearly thought was a ridiculous suggestion. "I'm a dragon, I'm not crazy. She's in no state to have a calm conversation, or she might just opt to vomit on me, and neither are desirable."

Susan placed the food on the table. "Man, that's cold. Not telling her she could get pregnant."

Everyone was shocked when Shilong said, "Humans and dragons are very prolific."

Everyone stared at Shilong except Gideon, who pulled the food towards him and started to dish up for himself.

Alice asked, "How'd you know that?"

Shilong said, "I know everything there is to know about dragons."

Gideon glanced up at Shilong and snorted before he started to shove food into his mouth. Alice definitely needed to talk to Gideon later about what he knew about the new passenger, as it was clear there was some history between the two. First, she would see how Hara was doing.

Alice found Hara in the privy. She had made it to the room before she had needed the bowl, which was upturned behind her. Pulling out a kerchief, Alice wet it with the water jug in the small room and passed it to Hara. Mumbling a thank you, Hara wiped her face then her mouth.

Leaning back against the wall, Alice waited for Hara to collect herself. "Are you upset that you're pregnant?"

Hara answered eventually. "I knew abstractly that being with Gideon involved the whole deal. Marriage, love, and even babies. Gideon has spoken about having kids, and that the ship would be an interesting place for them but I put that in the future."

She flapped her hand forward to demonstrate that she thought a long time in the future. Considering dragons lived for hundreds of years, Alice understood what Hara meant by "in the future": certainly not a few months after she and Gideon had been married.

Alice said, "There are some very good doctors here. I've heard they can even give you some herbs and then you wouldn't have to worry about a baby."

Hara shook her head without hesitation. "I'd never do that to Gideon. I know there are some women who would need that kind of thing but I'm in a different situation. I have a home and a means of employment and I'm sure Gideon will be a perfect housewife." Her voice was tinged with a sarcastic tone at the end.

Alice chuckled and Hara joined her laughter, though only softly. Hara looked pale again and Alice knew she was about to vomit. Alice leaned over and took the damp cloth from Hara's hand and rinsed it out and put it back in her hand. Hara mumbled a thank you.

Alice turned and realised Shilong had followed her out of the mess and was waiting for her in the corridor. She cleared her throat. "Ah, let me show you to your room."

Shilong bowed his head politely and followed her. Alice asked, "Will you have a lot of luggage?"

"All I own I have with me." He had a small bag over his shoulder. His clothes were rich and neat so she had assumed he would have a larger wardrobe, though it was undoubtedly easier to travel with less. She shrugged it off and opened the door to his room and motioned for him to enter.

He turned slowly around the room, studying the dimensions. He turned to her and his eyes burned with emotion. "Will you come in?"

Standing in the doorway, Alice answered. "I don't usually go into men's rooms."

His green eyes sparked with a deep green fire. None of that emotion showed on his face. He reminded her of a calm pool with untold depths. Alice was tempted to break her rule, as he was a truly handsome man. She had reason to be suspicious of handsome men.

"Would you allow me to court you?" Shilong asked.

"So polite, Mr Shilong." Alice smiled, amused by the question.

She turned to leave and he called after her. "That isn't a no."

She said over her shoulder, "No, that isn't a no." She let him take that how he wished.

Because their passenger didn't have any more luggage they could prepare for leaving the port. When Alice walked towards the bridge she could see Hara had recovered and moved off. No one else was on the bridge but they were most likely still in the mess, eating whatever Susan had prepared for lunch.

Alice went to the table that held the maps and leaned over it to set their course. She jumped back when something moved by the windows at the front of the bridge.

A creature made of metal sat calmly in the afternoon sun. It looked like a fat dog except it had a mane around its head like a lion's. It turned its head towards her with the whirr of gears. Not taking her eyes off the creature for even a moment she called to the rest of the ship. "Hey guys, I need someone up here with some guns. Big guns, preferably."

Murphy skidded onto the bridge with two of his guns already drawn. The clockwork dog-creature turned its head towards Murphy, who trained his guns on the creature. "Wow, what the heck is that?"

Shilong, who had come through the door after Murphy, said, "That's a foo-lion. It's a guardian of the summer palace in Yeijing. I'd not shoot it if I were you. They're very aggressive."

When Hara entered the bridge she asked, "What's it doing here?"

Angel glided onto the bridge and landed on the railing which ran under the windows. She chittered at the other clockwork creature. It turned to look at her and Shilong said, "They're servants to the Jade Dragon Empress. She probably sent it."

The foo-lion turned back its head from studying Angel to study the rest of the crew. It lifted a paw and rolled a metal tube forward which was decorated ornately with bas-relief. Everyone watched the tube roll towards them. Angel leaped off the railing and landed on the tube. She hopped a few times with it in her claws before she settled before Hara.

Murphy said, "I think she wants you to open it."

Leaning down to pick up the message tube, Hara hesitated when Alice said, "Wait. Is it safe?"

Murphy said, "The Han are famous for their poisons."

Shilong said, "It is unlikely the Empress would send one of her foo-lions to poison random airship captains." That wasn't a no either. Hara picked up the tube.

Gideon asked, "What does it say?"

"No idea, it's written in Han," Hara answered.

Shilong bowed his head respectfully. "If I may, it would be a pleasure for me to read it for you."

13

Hara passed him the scroll. "Are you Han, then?"

"You could say that. I have lived in Han for many years. Longer than anywhere else."

Opening the scroll, he read slowly, translating as he went. "The Jade Dragon, the Radiant Highness, the Lady of Ten Thousand Years and Empress of the Holy land of Han has invited the Lost Prince of the Wyvern Empire and his child bride to Yiheyuan, the Summer Palace, for a cordial visit at their earliest convenience."

Gideon asked, amused by the concept, "I'm a lost prince, am I?"

Hara looked at Gideon. "You don't look princely, but you do look a bit lost."

Gideon looked down at his professor like outfit. "Is that a comment about my clothes? The other professors were never very stylish so I dressed like them to fit in. I do have some other outfits which might be more appropriate for the summer palace but nothing besides this for the ship."

Hara shook her head. "You know me, I couldn't care less what you're wearing."

Gideon smiled at her. "So you aren't mad at me anymore for getting you pregnant?"

Hara narrowed her eyes, and Alice knew Hara still hadn't come to terms with her incipient motherhood and the role Gideon had played in it all.

Hara turned back to the scroll and said softly to herself, "A summons or an invite?"

Shilong said tactfully, "It would be an insult to the Empress if you didn't accept her invite, and her army and generals would see to it that you accepted."

Hara looked up a little shocked. "Would they really?"

Shilong bowed his head to indicate politely that her opinion outranked his own. Alice wondered if that was a

Han thing, as he appeared very self-effacing compared to the other men she knew.

Hara rolled up the scroll. "So either we have to take the long way home, or we go visit the Jade Dragon Empress."

Hara walked over to the map table and said to Alice, "See to our clearance to leave. I think we'd better start our journey now, as it might take a while to get home."

Alice looked at the foo-lion, who was still sitting calmly beneath the window. "What about that?"

Hara glanced at the clockwork creature. "If it wants to stay then I see no reason not to let it."

"It could be a spy."

Hara's lips moved in a slight smile. "Oh, I'm sure it is."

Alice assumed Hara had some plans for the clockwork creature which probably entailed a big drop and some ocean.

Angel hopped in front of the foo-lion and it slowly lowered its head to the small dragon. Angel placed her two front paws on either side of its face. Alice shook her head as she headed off the bridge. Neither one of the creatures was alive as they were made rather than born, but they indeed acted alive.

Alice realised quickly that Shilong was following her. She glanced over her shoulder. "We'll be leaving soon. You might want to take another airship, as it seems we aren't going through Han after all."

Shilong said, "I believe I will stay with the airship. I do like to travel, and you might need some help."

Alice snorted. "Hara doesn't need help. She's a force to be reckoned with. If the Empress forces Hara's hand she will learn to regret that decision."

They had passed his room and he still followed her. She said to Shilong, "I'm going to the port master's office. You don't have to follow me. Unless you remembered you actually have more luggage."

"I'll accompany you."

She shrugged. If he wanted to follow her around then that was fine with her. She wasn't going far, as the port master had an office nearby. It resembled an Empire clock tower, so it was easy to spot in the mostly traditional Nippon buildings that surrounded the port. Previously Alice had had a run in with the port master, so she knew what to expect when she went into the building.

The head port master pushed aside the teller at the window as she approached. She flashed him a warm smile, though it didn't reach her eyes. She was about to speak in the little Nipponese she had picked up while they had been in port when she remembered Shilong was still playing shadow. She had no idea if he knew Nipponese but his ease walking through the crowds of Nippon told her that he had been here for a while.

Alice waved to Shilong to step forward. "Translate for me, please."

He bowed his head slightly to acknowledge he would do as she wished. She was starting to enjoy that slight movement of acquiescence. She liked that he didn't argue with her or try to take over.

Alice said, "I require to leave port, immediately."

The port master carefully placed his hands on the desk. "The price for tariffs and fees is 60 gold yen."

Alice boiled with anger. That was twice as much as he would charge others in the port. Even Shilong frowned at the large amount.

"I only have 30 gold yen," Alice announced.

The port master was adamant. "It's 60 gold yen. If you want to leave this port in peace you'll have to pay the entire fee, gaikokujin." Alice had noticed recently the Nippon had been cold to foreigners. Especially those who came from the Wyvern Empire. It used to be anyone from the Wyvern Empire was welcomed everywhere, as they were good trade partners. Alice wasn't sure why there had been a change in recent years but she did know it made things difficult for her now.

Alice placed the money on the table. "Here is 30 gold yen. I will need a receipt but I'll have to go and get the rest from my ship."

The port master frowned at the suddenness of her capitulation. Shilong even opened his mouth to say something but decided silence was the better part of valor.

The port master hesitated then wrote out a receipt for the 30 gold yen. Alice bowed and thanked the man and left.

"He's a crook," Shilong growled.

Alice was amused he would be upset on her behalf. "I'm aware of that." The port master was not the first who thought he could trick her because she was a woman and a foreigner.

She walked with purpose as she needed to get to the other office before the port master could inform the staff there of his new price for their departure. The port was a large place and so they had smaller offices of the port authority at either end for convenience.

Skipping up the stairs, Alice entered the smaller office. She bowed to the single man who sat on the floor with his small desk. He frowned at her but otherwise kept his thoughts to himself. Alice smiled warmly and this time it reached her eyes. She really did like getting back at small-minded idiots like the port master. She handed over the receipt. "I need a pass. I've paid, see."

The teller inspected the receipt and pulled some papers towards himself as he filled out the documents she would need in order to leave. She thanked the man and bounced out of the office.

Shilong said, "That was clever."

The shocked tone of his voice offended her a little, so when she spoke it was sharp. "I told you, I read."

"I see." He sounded suitably chastised.

Alice waved her pass to the men in charge of untying the airship and took the rope ladder back up as it was quicker than the lift. When she got back to the bridge she found Hara had set a course that would take them around Han.

Alice looked around for the foo-lion and found it curled up in the sun below the windows with Angel sleeping on top of it. Maybe they weren't going to be rid of the foo-lion after all.

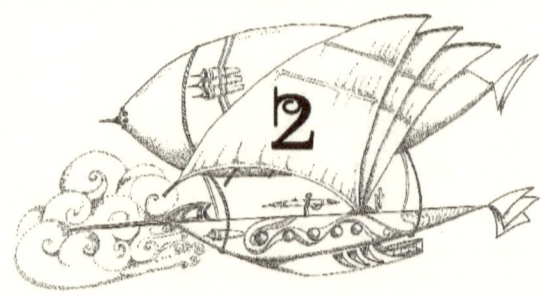

They had no trouble getting out of Nippon. Alice leant against the helm and watched the clouds pass. It appeared like a storm might hit later, as dark, angry clouds crowded the sky. All it meant at the moment was that they had good tail wind. If this weather held up they would reach the Ma-i islands faster than expected.

There was a small Wyvern Empire colony in the Mai-i islands where they could resupply before they took the long way back, probably through the Middle East, which held its own troubles. The area had been war-torn as far back as memory recalled.

A shadow flickered over the bow of the airship. Either it was a very large bird or it was trouble. While Alice was squinting, trying to make out what the shadow was, Shilong came onto the bridge. "It seems we're making good time."

The shadow flickered again over the Blazing Blunderbuss. It moved wrong for a bird. Was it a dragon? All humans were always conscious of shadows. They had lived too long with the menace of the dragons to all of a sudden put aside their fears after the treaty had been signed.

A huge airship came out of the angry clouds Alice had been admiring before. She swore under her breath.

Shilong asked, "Do you think they're hostile?"

"Yes." Those shadows had to be gliders or scouts of some sort. Worse, they might have a dragon of their own. Outside of the Wyvern Empire many dragons worked for themselves rather than for the government. Even in Han, where the dragons ruled, not all dragons were associated with the government.

Alice rang the bell to announce danger. The clang echoed throughout the ship. Murphy skidded onto the bridge and stumbled to the weapons console Hara had made for him so he could shoot all the guns on the ship from one place. He started spinning wheels and turning levers.

He growled, "Where are you, bastards?" A glider came into view in front of them. It was made of beige concertina wings that were massive compared to the small man it was carrying.

The Blazing Blunderbuss shuddered as something blew up too close to them.

Alice yelled, "Murphy! Give them some trouble now before they take us down without a fight."

Murphy grumbled, "I would if the blighters would just stay still."

Alice growled, "Sure, I'll just ask them nicely. Just shoot, Murphy."

Shilong grabbed onto one of the railings on the helm as the ship rocked sideways from Alice's manoeuvres. "Do you think we'll get out of this?" he asked.

Before Alice could answer, Gideon and Hara arrived on the deck. Alice wasn't sure what had taken them so long but decided it wasn't the time to ask.

Hara said, "Make us difficult to hit. Those look like gliders and they're trying to board us. Gideon?"

She turned to the dragon and he said, "Onto it. Those gliders are difficult to catch. They're made with dragons in mind. I can go after them or after the airship but not both. Which?"

"The airship. We'll deal with the boarders," Hara said, concern clear in her voice. They weren't set up to fight off a large boarding party. If the airship got close enough they could board the Blazing Blunderbuss with dozens of men and the crew would be hopelessly outnumbered.

Gideon kissed Hara on her cheek and left. Hara said, "Murphy, you're the first line. Take Talen with you. Tell the girls to lock themselves in a room."

Liam would stay in engineering and make sure they had more than enough power to manoeuvre. Alice was taking evasive actions. Hopefully they could prevent the gliders from landing on the ship.

Another blast came nearby and the ship swung in the air with a shudder. Hara turned to Alice and opened her mouth to say something when a man barrelled onto the bridge. Hara lifted her gun up but the man moved fast enough that he kicked her gun out of her grip before she could aim and shoot.

Moving quickly, Shilong pulled him off Hara, then flipped him over his hip and onto the floor. Before he could finish the invader off, two other men came onto the bridge. Either there were a lot more gliders than Alice had seen before, or they were formidable fighters and had gotten past Murphy and Talen. There was a good chance the two men were already dead.

Hara and Shilong engaged the two fighters who were on the bridge. Alice concentrated on flying the ship. There was still a chance that the other ship could board them.

2

Hara wasn't much of a fighter. She used gadgets rather than brute force, so she was getting knocked around a bit. Alice tried to time her course corrections to help Hara. Shilong, graceful as a cat on his feet, moved to intercept the invaders' attacks. Nothing Alice did bothered Shilong.

Murphy roared as he charged onto the deck. Blood poured from a wound on his head and he had no weapons. He lowered his shoulder and took down one of the attackers with a tackle to his body. Hara managed to throw one of her net balls at the downed man and a light net shot out and covered the man and trapped him for the time being. Murphy stumbled back to avoid being trapped as well. He didn't let it distract him for long and he turned to fight the other invaders.

Murphy, Hara and Shilong fought with two of the invaders. Another must have come onto the bridge without Alice noticing, as the next thing she knew there was a blade pressed to her throat.

Alice wondered why they didn't kill her. There were two reasons to keep the crew alive. One was they wanted to rape the women and preferred if they were alive, but since they had also left Murphy alive that was unlikely. Alice knew it was more likely these were slavers rather than pirates.

There was no way to negotiate with the man holding the blade to her throat as there was a good chance he didn't speak any language she knew. Alice lifted her hands slowly off the wheel of the helm. The man put a hand on her arm but he was jerked away from her so forcefully that his blade cut into her chin.

Alice slapped her hand to her chin. Blood oozed through her fingers and she applied more pressure to stop the bleeding. The blood didn't worry her as the cut

3

could have been worse. She put her other free hand on the helm and spun it to move them away from the other airship.

Shilong fought with the man who had almost cut her throat. They had a similar fighting style, both using their whole bodies. They kicked and blocked with their arms so concisely that no true blow got through. There was no extra movement that wasn't needed. It reminded Alice of dancers rather than fighters.

The slaver lunged with his blade. Alice spun the helm quickly and the Blazing Blunderbuss tilted at the sudden course change. The slaver stumbled and missed Shilong, which allowed him to tackle and throw the slaver over his hip. The slaver slammed into the map table and crumbled to the floor.

Alice looked at the others. Murphy sat on top of one of the slavers. He puffed with the effort to keep the man down. The man had no weapons so he must have put up a fight purely with his fists. She had no idea where Talen was. Hara fought with another of the slavers but she wasn't winning. The one that was in the net sawed away with a blade.

Alice dared not leave her post at the helm to take on the downed man in the net. If one of the slavers got hold of the helm they would be able to steer the ship where the other airship could board them easily, and then they would be completely outnumbered. If the fighters were anything like these men then they didn't have a chance if that happened. She had to keep flying erratically in order to keep them from becoming pretty slaves for some flesh master.

Shilong turned and kicked out and knocked the man in the net unconscious, then took on the man attacking Hara.

Talen stumbled onto the bridge. He had blood coming from several cuts and it was clear he had taken the brunt of the attack when the slavers had boarded.

The airship lurched as it suddenly lost power. Alice was thrown against the wheel and had to hold on tight not to end up on the floor. Hara smacked against the wall and slumped down. She appeared dazed and stayed there for a moment blinking her eyes rapidly.

Alice yelled, "Liam!"

Murphy looked up from the man he had tied up. There was only one reason to lose power so abruptly. The boarders had managed to get to engineering and were interfering with the engines. Murphy leapt to his feet and pelted out of there. Usually Angel was in the engine room and hopefully she was there with her foo-lion. They would be able to distract the men from hurting Liam.

They would want Liam as much as they wanted the women. A smart, handsome young man would go on the slave market for as much as a young woman.

Alice turned the wheel on the helm again. The Blazing Blunderbuss responded sluggishly but there was enough wind in the sails for the basic movement. This time it brought the slaver airship into view. Gideon, as a massive golden dragon, sat on top of the envelope. He tore into it like a two-year-old into a birthday cake.

Men were climbing up the lines to reach him, and if they did they would do some damage, but Gideon had the advantage when it came to airships. He could fly and they couldn't. They wouldn't risk falling off as it was a long way down to the ocean below—far enough that it would be like hitting something solid rather than liquid.

An explosion came from the slaver's airship and it tilted to one side. Gideon had ignited one of the cavities

5

that held the flammable gas which kept the ship up in the air. He spread open his wings and the wind pulled him sharply away from the floundering ship.

The slavers struggled to move the ship around and away from Gideon as the explosion had set the envelope on fire, and if they didn't put it out soon it would take out another pocket and they would go down in flames.

Alice didn't have to worry about the slaver airship except to avoid it so that the burning pieces fluttering from it didn't land on the Blazing Blunderbuss. She moved them away but that meant she could no longer see the airship or Gideon. Liam still hadn't gotten the engine going so it was a painfully slow manoeuvre.

Hara had her gun trained on the downed men who were tied up. She rubbed the back of her head absently but she was no long dazed by her collision with the wall. Shilong was tying up the last man. He came up to Alice. He did not look like a man who had just been in a fight for his life. His clothes were tugged into place and he looked as if he were ready to meet the Empress.

Shilong picked up her hand that had blood on it. He turned it over then tilted her head up so he could see the wound. His voice was rough. "You're injured."

Talen snarled. "Yeah, so are most of us. Those buggers had some moves on them." Shilong did not even look towards Talen. Talen leaned against the wall but he was still on his feet so he couldn't be too bad.

Murphy came onto the bridge. "Sorted the fella down in the engine room. What're we gonna to do with them?" He didn't need to announce his success in saving Liam, as the engines kicked in and everyone swayed as the Blazing Blunderbuss started moving again.

Hara said, "We're not too far away from some islands. We'll go lower and drop them off into the ocean and they can swim."

Murphy said, "You know they're almost certainly slavers."

Hara agreed. "Doesn't mean we have to be as evil as they are. Alice, go get Hermia. She'll need to see to Talen before he gets worse."

Talen looked pale so Alice hoped he hadn't lost too much blood. Even if she didn't like the man, she didn't wish him dead.

Shilong caught her arm. "You rest, I'll get the physician."

Hermia was likely locked up in her room. She had no real fighting skills and the slavers would have used her against them if she had been taken. If it had been pirates they would have just killed her and moved on. She could stay safely in her room until the fighting was over, and then she could be useful.

Alice nodded her thanks to Shilong and leant back against the helm. She looked to the others. "That was close."

The airship dipped as Gideon landed on the deck at the rear of the airship. He usually tried to sneak in but if he was weary from the fight he would save his energy and just hold the ship while he shifted himself back into a human shape before climbing on over the railing.

Gideon had explained to her once how the dragons transformed. Apparently on their home planet they shifted mass in between planes all the time. Alice didn't understand how it all worked, only that it did work and that dragons had travelled from their own planet to this one in a blink of an eye.

Despite the fact Alice liked to read, she was more interested in the human race and the people around the world than in how things, which were so small that you couldn't see them, worked.

* * *

The bleeding on Alice's chin had almost stopped by the time Hermia had finished with Talen and finally had time to see to the wound. Alice sat on her bunk while Hermia opened her physician's case. It had been a present from the doctors Hermia had been studying with in Nippon.

Hermia was a very different girl from the noblewoman who had run away from an arranged marriage and had fallen into a plot to try to take over the Empire. Hermia had recovered well from that incident. Now she was a trained doctor, most likely better trained than any doctor back in the Empire.

Hermia was technically fostered out to Gideon, but the dragon hardly noticed the woman was on the ship. He saw anyone on board to be in Hara's collection and therefore her responsibility. Dragons had a strange way of looking at responsibility.

Hermia tilted her head up. "You know you almost died. If he'd known what he was doing he could've cut the carotid artery."

Alice thought back to that moment when she had felt the blade on her throat and she had been sure she was dead. There had been no hesitation in the slaver's motions. He had put blades to a lot of throats. "Oh, he knew what he was doing. Shilong stopped him. He already had the blade to my throat. This is actually not too bad."

Wetting a cloth, Hermia wiped away the blood to better see the wound. "Mmmm, and wounds like this always bleed like a geyser. This is over the bone and gaping a bit so I'll need to put in some stitches, although the cut isn't too bad. I'm better now at stitches; you won't even have a scar."

Playing with her bag, Hermia brought out potions and other tools she would need. As she worked, Hermia asked, "What's the passenger like? I was asleep when he came on board, so I missed the introductions. Is he Nipponese or something? Susan says he looks like a local."

"I think he's Han. From the name alone."

"Oh, the name?" Hermia was curious but she was also sidetracked by her work. Alice appreciated being distracted from her own wound, so continued the conversation.

"Shilong is a Han name. Many of their people have 'long' in their surnames or their first names. He also recognised the foo-lion."

"Ah, the creature Angel was riding around the airship today." Angel had been riding the foo-lion everywhere, stroking her small claws through his carved metal hair occasionally.

"Yes, the two of them seem to get along well. I think Hara would be jealous if she wasn't so upset about being pregnant." Alice wasn't sure if it was a good idea to encourage the friendship, but Angel had always been Hara's responsibility.

Hermia looked up sharply from her work. "How'd I miss that?" Alice didn't feel so bad about missing the pregnancy if their resident doctor had also managed to miss the signs.

"It was Susan. She noticed Hara was having morning sickness. I didn't notice until she pointed it out and then it was obvious."

9

"If I'd been around, I would've noticed. How is she taking it? I have herbs, you know." Hermia winced when she said the last. She didn't like the idea, but as a good doctor she wouldn't stop anyone from having the best of her care.

Alice shook her head just the slightest bit because Hermia was still cleaning out the wound with little dabs of something that stung and she didn't want to move too much. "No, I talked to her. It's just the shock. I think she wants kids. I think it's the idea of raising little versions of Gideon that is freaking her out."

"Mmmm, and hybrids are interesting."

Hermia would be familiar with hybrid human-dragons, as she had once lived at court with her parents, who were related to the Emperor. "You're a noble; you would've been around hybrids. What are they like?"

Hermia tilted Alice's head back more and started with the stitches as she spoke. "They're very much like dragons. Don't age very quickly. They take thirty years-plus to reach maturity. Once they do they don't seem to age at all. They have golden eyes like the dragons, and you know that making stuff 'poof' into existence? Well, they can do that as well. I've never seen any of them change into a dragon but there are rumours that some of them can. I think the changing is a throwback."

Alice winced at the little pinch of each stitch. Hermia had put something on her skin to numb it a bit but it wasn't infallible.

"If what Gideon told me is true, then the making things 'poof' is related to the changing into a dragon thing," Alice added as a way to direct her own mind away from the sharp needle piercing her skin.

Hermia looked up at Alice, the needle raised in one hand. "Oh, really? Then I think they can all change. They must be trying to keep it low-key. If humans realised dragons could have dragons with human mates then they would freak. At the moment all they see is weird-looking humans and it doesn't freak them out nearly as much."

Hermia went back to stitching. Alice asked, "Would you have married one of the dragons?"

Hermia didn't even hesitate as she answered. "In a heartbeat. That's what everyone at court wanted more than anything else. Marry a dragon, and if you can't marry a dragon then a first or second generation hybrid. After that, humans with screeds of money or land."

"I mean, would you really want to be with a dragon? They're so different. This whole collecting thing." Alice wanted to shake her head but Hermia wasn't finished.

"They call it collecting, but it's actually something more complex. Dragons see themselves as part of a bigger whole—more holistic than we humans see ourselves. Dragons are what they collect. If a dragon collects weapons he is violent. If he collects money then he's materialistic. Most dragons collect people because it means they have empathy. It wasn't always a desirable trait among dragons. In the early days they used to collect human heads instead. I prefer this way of collecting things."

"Doesn't it smack of slavery? I can tell you if those guys who attacked us today had their way we would be locked up in a cage." Alice had been watching Gideon with Hara, and she wondered if it was just Gideon that was different or if he was typical of all dragons.

"Dragons believe that if you're to keep your belongings in a cage then you don't deserve them. A dragon won't have a vault; instead he'll spend hours polishing everything he owns. Other dragons won't steal something that's highly polished. If it's stained or broken

11

they'll take it in a snap. They believe if you aren't willing to look after something then you don't deserve it."

"So dragons can divorce?" This concept astonished Alice. Humans couldn't divorce unless they jumped through dozens of hoops and women never instigated it. If they did manage to get a divorce then the women were ostracised, as people wondered why a man would put her aside. No one thought it might be the man that had a flaw.

Hermia chuckled and finished off with the last stitch. "Yes, and it's a huge stigma for the dragon who is left by its mate. For a woman to leave means the dragon must have done something wrong." At least that was the same for humans. There was such disgrace for divorced people, they often moved to the countryside.

"What if the woman is just a gold digger?" Alice was curious about this. Humans made mistakes all the time over who they should marry and dragons were rumoured to choose their brides very quickly.

"Well, the dragon is rich. She'll stay for the money. The dragon will just collect more money for her. He wouldn't care if she was sleeping with someone else if he collected a gold digger. It was his fault in the first place to collect a woman who wanted nothing but his gold. See how that reflects on the dragon rather than on the woman? Dragons are very picky about who they mate with. It might seem like they make snap choices, as they often fall in love at first sight, but it isn't actually anything like that at all. They have been studying humans for years. They know a good egg when they see one." That made sense.

Hermia packed away her gear as she spoke. "The women they tend to mate with are smart and resourceful. The kind who are loyal. Someone who reflects who the dragon is himself." Hermia snapped her case closed. "You should be good as new in a few days."

"Do I have to take it easy?" Alice gingerly touched the stitches. Her chin was still a little numb from whatever Hermia had put on it.

Hermia waved off her concern for her wound. "That would be useful but not essential. Are you thinking of doing any extraneous activity?" Hermia's eyes lit up and she asked, "With the Han guy? Susan said he was good-looking."

Alice shook her head and Hermia frowned. "Why not? Are you not attracted to him?"

"It isn't that. What would people think?" Alice knew it was a silly excuse, but she had been forced to leave her hometown because her suitor had spread rumours about her, so she knew it could be very uncomfortable if rumours started up again. It wouldn't take much for her to be ostracised on a ship that had fewer than a dozen people.

Hermia sniffed. "If that's the only thing stopping you, then you should take him to your bed." Alice had known it was only an excuse rather than a reason.

Sighing, Alice leaned back against the wall by her bed. "I wish I could have a forever kind of thing, but living here on Blazing Blunderbuss makes it almost impossible. I don't want to leave, either. I love my work and I get to see the world. It's my dream. If I could have someone to share it with me, like Hara has Gideon, then it would be perfect."

"How will you know it can't be a forever kind of thing with this man? We're taking the long way back to the Empire, so he'll be with us for a while. There's clearly something on this ship that's making him willing to stick it out with us, even if we're avoiding the Jade Empress by heading in the opposite direction from Han."

"I don't know. What if he isn't interested at all?"

Hermia picked up her bag and stood ready to leave. "If that's true, he isn't worth your effort in the first place. Fortune favours the bold." With this trite advice Hermia gave her a mock salute and left her room.

Alice tilted her head back and closed her eyes. Would she dare to have the courage to let a man court her?

Alice wasn't sure what she was doing. It was late and she had the early shift on the bridge, so she really should be resting and not standing outside Shilong's door. Gently resting her forehead on the wood beside the door, Alice whispered words of encouragement to herself.

Eventually, she straightened and knocked softly on the door. Only after she had knocked did she wonder if he was already in bed. She wouldn't want to disturb him. It was too late to take back the soft knock. If he was asleep maybe she could just walk away and no one would even know she had been knocking at the passenger's door.

Alice had convinced herself he didn't intend to answer and was half-turned when the door opened. Shilong, dressed in more traditional clothes for sleeping, paused when he realised it was her at the door. He wore a silk buttoned shirt and sleep trousers that fitted him awfully well. Alice was staring, so she apologised. "I'm sorry, I didn't mean to wake you."

Shilong had his hair loose. It was almost as long as her own and very straight. "I was just preparing for bed. Is there something you need?"

He did not act upset at all that she was knocking on his door so late in the evening.

Alice blushed and took a step back. "It's nothing. A silly idea, really."

Shilong tilted his head as he took her in. He stepped back, inviting her in silently. Alice couldn't move forward or backwards. Finally Shilong said kindly, "Do you wish to come in?"

Chewing on her bottom lip Alice nodded her head. She felt like a fool. Shilong was obviously a well-travelled, worldly person; he would not want someone like her in his room. She had come from a small provincial town on the edge of the Wyvern Empire. Her only experience with the rest of the world came from books and her recent travel with the Blazing Blunderbuss.

Shilong offered his hand. The gesture startled her, as people from the East rarely touched others and certainly not strangers. She placed her hand in his and let out the breath she had been keeping in.

He pulled her slowly into his room. He said, "What brings you here, wo de ai ren?"

She blushed. "Well, you said...I thought..."

He brought her over to his bed. He sat down and pulled her down as well so she was sitting on the edge of his bed next to him. She expected him to start undressing her. She knew when she had knocked on his door so late that there was only one thing she wanted.

But he didn't do anything. He just held her hand. Alice shifted nervously. Eventually she said, "Should I...ummm, do anything? I mean, you said I should...I assumed you were flirting with me." She blushed as she said the last. She felt like a bumbling teenager.

Shilong tightened his grip on her hand briefly before he said. "I know what I said, but I wish to hear the words

16

from you, so I know you're here because you wish to be here."

"Oh."

Alice actually liked that. Too many men assumed she wanted a bed mate. That was one of her issues with Talen. He had assumed, because there were no other single men on board who weren't gangly or gun-happy, she would be desperate to be in his bed.

She took in a breath to say something but then she realised she wasn't sure why she was here. She held her breath for a moment as she thought of what to say.

Dizzy, she finally decided she would just have to be honest. She slowly let out the breath she was holding and relaxed a little. "I'm lonely."

"That's not a good reason to go to a man's bedroom, wo de ai ren." His voice was gentle with understanding. She could hear the echo of his own loneliness in his voice.

She shrugged. He wasn't wrong and she couldn't disagree with him so she thought she would try to explain. Maybe saying it out loud would settle her thoughts. "You see, Hara's amazing. She took me on though there were horrible rumours about me. She didn't seem to care and she taught me everything she knows about airships and I love that. I don't want to leave the Blazing Blunderbuss, but that does mean I'm limited in who I can socialise with. I mean romantically. Murphy is alright but he isn't my type. Besides, he has Susan. Liam is way too young and Talen…well, Talen is an ass. So that leaves me alone and lonely."

Reaching out between them, Shilong picked up both her hands. He laid them in his lap and clasped them between his. She liked the warmth of him.

"I understand," he said carefully.

17

"Thank you. I was really nervous. I don't do things like this."

"At all?" he asked with a single eyebrow going up.

She furrowed her brow in confusion. Then she realised he was asking gently if she had ever been with a man before. Her first love had betrayed her and she had never gotten past kisses. He had told everyone she was a whore when she wouldn't sleep with him. She had thought they had a future together and all he had wanted was to get under her skirt. Alice knew she didn't want a short fling even if Shilong was unbearably handsome and considerate.

Getting to her feet, Alice pulled her hands from his grasp. "I think this was a bad idea. I'm sorry. I really am."

He didn't try to stop her. He just looked up at her. "What do you fear?"

She ran her now sweating hands down her skirt. "I had a beau once. I wanted a future. Children, the lot, but he just wanted fleeting pleasure. I don't want that. I want something more permanent. Something that will last forever."

Shilong tilted his head as he studied her. It reminded her of Angel or Gideon when they were studying something new and interesting. Shilong offered his hand again. "I can offer you that, if you give me a chance."

Alice hesitated. She looked at his hand for a very long time. He didn't drop it, instead reaching further and picking up her own.

He said, "What do you wish, wo de ai ren? What dream can I offer to you this night to entice you?"

"You'll do anything I want? Stop, if I ask?" It wasn't just about loneliness. She really wanted that connection with another human being that told her she wasn't alone in the world. Intimacy.

"This is your night. Of course, I'll do anything you wish." His voice was rough as he spoke.

"Then make love to me," she said determinedly. Hermia was right: she needed to decide what she wanted and go for it.

He growled softly in the back of his throat and pulled her closer against him. It was the first time his emotion had broken his façade. Alice surrendered to the moment, embracing the touch, the feel of everything around her. It was a dream-like experience, which she attributed to the fact that he was exquisitely patient.

Alice lay beneath him and she knew it was almost that moment when there would be no going back. They had taken their time to get to this point. Shilong was above her and he hesitated. His long black hair cascaded around his face. It was no longer perfectly straight. She had been running her hands through the silky length and she could see the passage of her fingers. His green eyes were like sharp emeralds, barely visible in the dim light of the lantern.

Shilong's voice when he spoke was choked with emotion. "Give me your hands, wo de tai tai."

Alice moved her hands from his back so he could grasp them. He moved them above her head. He bent down and laid soft butterfly kisses on her cheek and mouth. He said hoarsely, "I always wanted it to be like this. Entwined like this."

Alice was curious about the words. "Is this your first time, as well?"

"Yes, wo de ai ren." He must be exaggerating. Maybe he meant that this was his first time with someone who was a complete novice. Alice planned to ask him to clarify when a sharp pain pierced her lower back. She yelped and Shilong kissed her lips.

He said distractedly, "This won't hurt. I'll be gentle, wo de ai ren, I'll be gentle."

She asked, "What does that mean, the wo de airy thing?"

"It means my lover," he answered as he lowered his lips to hers.

She really was his lover.

***

Hara found Hermia in her room. She was reading something, but it must have been confusing as she was frowning at the text. She put the book down when Hara entered.

She jumped up. "Captain."

"I'm not here as your captain, I'm here as a freaked-out person. I'm an aberration. I'm going to push out a bloody monster." Hara waved her hands over her stomach to indicate she meant the pregnancy.

Hermia laughed and stopped suddenly when she saw Hara wasn't even vaguely joking. Closing the space between them, Hermia took up Hara's hands and brought her over to the bed. There was not enough furniture in the room for both of them to sit on chairs and Hara was used to using the beds as chairs in the small quarters.

Hara let out a breath. "Am I overreacting?"

"Most likely, but that is your prerogative. I'm not surprised you're freaking out. You only got used to the idea of having Gideon in your life. You might take as long to get used to the idea of a child."

Hara grunted. "If that's the case then the kid might be talking before I get used to the idea of being a mother." Hara had been reluctant to even entertain the idea of a relationship with Gideon and had kept him at arm's length for months. It had only been when she had been shot and dying that she had changed her mind. Even then, it had taken her a while to realise that Gideon wasn't like all the other men in her life and that he was actually trustworthy. The thing that had changed everything, though, was when she had realised he loved her. Marrying Gideon had saved her life, as she was able to heal like a dragon did now.

Hermia had kept Hara's hands, and Hara didn't want to admit that she was glad for the connection to another human being. She let out a breath and asked Hermia, "Is it going to be awful?"

"Not at all. The mortality rate for dragon children is almost nil, and when there is a death it's typically because of accidents instead of anything involved in the birthing process. The mothers never die. Dragons can manipulate the cells in a person's body, and while their mate gives birth that's all they're focused on."

Hara shuddered. "I'm trying not to think about that part of this whole mess. It's far enough away."

"Not as far away as you think. Dragon foetuses tend to grow at a greater rate than human babies. At the moment though, it's probably only this big." Hermia demonstrated the size with her thumb and forefinger.

Hara stared at the seemingly tiny size of her child. "It's only the size of a bean," she said incredulously.

Hermia shrugged. "If it was a bean made from something squishy like jelly. I mean, the baby is small but it's made of flesh and blood just like you."

Hara almost put her hand on her stomach but resisted the urge. She hadn't expected to be a mother so soon, but she wasn't averse to the idea.

Hermia seemed to understand her thoughts, as she said, "You'll make a very good mother and Gideon will be the best of fathers. This child will be a very lucky child to have you two as parents."

Hara grew fierce as she thought of her father. There was no way she would let her child be used like she had been used when she was a child. Hara's father was a conman and only saw people as victims, including his own daughter.

Hermia was right. This was a lucky child. When Hara left Hermia's room she found Talen waiting to talk to her. She had wondered when he would put in his two cents'. Hara leaned on the wall next to him and waited for him to collect himself. He took his time but she was patient.

Eventually he said, "Your father would be disappointed in you."

Hara might have taken that personally a month or two previously, but she was more confident about her past now. Instead, she smiled. "Thanks, I needed to hear that." Talen frowned, so she explained, "If my dad approved of something I did, I'd stop doing it. Well, maybe, but my father is the last thing on my mind."

Talen grumbled. "So you're happy you're going to spawn a monster?"

Hara looked at him carefully. Talen was a friend—or he had been at a time when she had needed someone. Now she had other people in her life. She had hoped Talen would be able to fit in her life now, but he became surlier every day.

Hara closed the space between them. "Talen, you might say stuff about me, but you aren't to say a thing about my kid. Are we clear?" Her cold voice made Talen straighten.

She patted his cheek. "Think about where you want to be, Talen, and remember this is my home. This is what I want."

She left him and hoped he would make the right choice.

<hr />

The storm had really hit when Alice woke for her shift. She slipped out of Shilong's bed carefully, so as not to wake him. He mumbled and rolled over. She dressed quickly and rushed back to her room to get ready for her shift. The storm made the airship wobble like a drunken sailor so she held onto the railing that ran along the narrow corridor.

Her back was tender but she wasn't sure why. It wasn't like Shilong had been rough with her. She would see Hermia later for some tea, as her back wasn't the only thing that smarted a bit. The other bits—well, she knew why they hurt. But those hurts were easily put out of mind as they weren't really that painful.

Hara was at one of the other stations when Alice arrived on the bridge. Alice could see why. The storm outside appeared vicious. Hara was doubtlessly battening down the hatches the true Hara way, which meant pushing levers that sent signals to pneumatic pistons to close hatches and shutters. It did mean they didn't have to hire a young lad who would clamber on the outside of the airship to ready it for a storm. For repairs Liam did have to climb the ropes, but he saw that as a vacation from the engineering room where he spent most of his time.

Hara glanced over her shoulder and smiled when Alice entered the bridge. "Morning. You look good." She frowned. "What's that on your cheek?"

Hermia really had done a good job on the stitches as Alice only vaguely felt the pain of the cut. "It's nothing."

Hara shrugged. "I'll check the rest is stowed away. These storms can get violent extremely quickly. You keep her on course as much as possible, but there'll inevitably be drift with these kinds of winds."

Alice felt like she needed to speak to someone and Hara was the only one who was in a relationship that resembled one Alice really wanted. "Hara?"

Hara stopped at the door of the bridge and turned back. "Yes?"

Alice chewed on her lip for a moment. "I know we've talked about me getting into a relationship."

Hara had once promised Alice she would set her up with someone.

Hara raised an eyebrow. "I take it you and the passenger have hit it off. What are you worried about? That the others on the Blazing Blunderbuss will treat you like the villagers did when your ex spread rumours about you?"

Alice let out a breath. "Yes. I know it's stupid, because Susan is staying with Murphy and you know she isn't intending to always be in that relationship. No one has bothered her."

Hara smiled. "I think you've answered your own question."

She had, and she smiled at Hara. "Thank you. You should head to bed soon. Your baby needs you to be rested."

Hara rolled her eyes. "It's a jelly bean to me at this stage." She left on that cryptic note, and Alice decided she really should learn more about anatomy.

The weather was fierce enough that Alice really didn't have much time to think about her new relationship with Shilong, as the storm took all of her concentration.

Shilong arrived on the bridge around dawn. He studied the storm. "How are we?"

"Safe enough. This ship is built to take even weather like this. It just isn't pretty."

Shilong stepped behind her and laid something around her neck. Her hand went up to it and she could feel it was a necklace. She glanced down to see it was made up of green jade beads and a pendant of something carved. She picked up the pendant and looked at it closely. It appeared as if two dragons were twisted around each other as they flew through the sky.

Alice said, a little stunned by the gift, "This is lovely. Is it for me?"

He kissed her cheek. Considering they were alone on the bridge she didn't say anything, though she was a little uncomfortable with affection being shown in a place where anyone could walk in on them. She would have thought a Han would be more circumspect in his displays of affection.

Shilong said as he came to stand beside the helm, "I carved it myself. This particular jade is a hard stone so it takes a long time to carve. It is the twin to one I have from childhood. A totem."

Alice asked distractedly, "A totem? I haven't heard of those before. What is it?"

His voice was warm with emotion as he spoke, "It's just something that reminds me of home. If I ever want to go back all I have to do is hold it in my hand and wish to be home and it transports me there in the twinkling of an eye."

Alice smiled at the thought of something that had such strong connotations of home. She had some letters from her mother that always reminded her of home. It warmed Alice that he would give her something that was a copy of something so important to him. It connected them.

Alice tucked the pendant under her collar. "I wish I had something to give you."

He shrugged. "You have already blessed me."

Alice blushed. "About that. I don't think we should be so…so demonstrative around the rest of the crew."

Shilong frowned. She could tell he wasn't pleased with her request.

He asked, "You'll come to my room tonight?"

She nodded, a blush warming her ears. She had enjoyed their time together and she didn't want that to end any time soon.

He relaxed. "Yes, that might be prudent."

Alice looked around to make sure they were alone and leaned forward to kiss him. He lightly touched her hair then dropped his hand. Alice was sure people would gossip about her and Shilong, and she just wanted to avoid anything awkward. Particularly from the men. She would hate for Talen to reassert his advances if he realised she was sleeping with Shilong.

Alice turned her attention back to the storm and occasionally touched the pendant under her collar. By the time the storm had blown out its temper her shift was almost over, and she knew they were off course when she saw land instead of sea below them.

Alice said to Shilong, who had stayed with her through her whole shift, "Can you please get Hara? I think she will want to see this." He bowed his head in gentlemanly politeness and left her on the bridge.

If she had asked Murphy to do the same thing, he would have yelled down the corridor. Hara didn't take long but it was long enough for the smudge Alice had seen on the horizon to solidify into three airships.

Hara went up to the window of the bridge. "Please tell me that isn't the Han military."

Alice kept silent. She had been out there with the telescope and knew what would be obvious soon. The Han airships had crafted dragons on the helms of their ships. The envelopes of the gas above them were a bright green with a stylized dragon curled in a circle stencilled on the side.

Hara glanced back. "How off course are we?"

"We're on the border. I assume they were blown off course as well."

"Our bad luck then." Hara went to the voice tube that led to engineering. She called down, "Liam send up that foo-lion, thank you."

The Han airships surrounded them. Hara stayed on the bridge at the window to watch for the flags. The ships signalled that they intended to board. Alice had already known that and had brought the Blazing Blunderbuss to an almost complete standstill. There were still winds from the fading storm. It meant the crossing would be tricky for anyone that came over, but not impossible. They were being polite if they were crossing over instead of insisting Hara go over to one of their ships. Or maybe they wanted to have the men on board just in case they had to take over the Blazing Blunderbuss.

Hara had most of the crew come up to the bridge to make sure there weren't any misunderstandings. Liam would stay in engineering just in case they needed power unexpectedly.

Shilong, standing next to Alice, asked, "What do you think the captain will do?"

"She'll go to Han. She won't want to put the crew at risk, so she'll bite the bullet and go visit the Han Empress. Though I think she's tired of being yanked around by arrogant rulers and she even liked the Emperor of the Wyvern Empire. So there might be something to her reluctance, but she won't put us at risk."

Shilong nodded his head in understanding. "She looks after her collection."

Alice glanced at him. "That's a very dragon concept."

"We live in a world where dragons are the top of the food chain. I'm surprised there aren't more dragon concepts in the human consciousness."

Alice was curious about this. She had always assumed the fact that dragons didn't talk to humans much explained why there wasn't more of the dragon culture in the human population. They were certainly close-mouthed about their heritage and knowledge in the Wyvern Empire. It was accepted that dragons were superior beings, and when asked for some of their knowledge they would say something along the lines of, "It's better for a world to grow into its own." Alice had no idea what they meant by that. Besides, they were stingy with their technological advances.

Shilong said, "I'm not sure if they'll recognise me."

Alice glanced at him. "Is that going to be a problem?"

"They might insist that I go with them."

Alice sniffed. "Not going to happen."

He raised an eyebrow at her confidence. She explained. "Hara won't let them. I told you, she looks after the crew and that includes passengers."

He bowed his head, accepting her words. The bridge was tense as they waited for the contingent from the Han ship to arrive. The foo-lion sat by Hara's feet with Angel sitting on his shoulder. Her little claw curled up in the metal plated mane around his head.

When the soldiers came in, they had rifles on their shoulders and they glanced around to see if the crew was going to be difficult before they took up parade stances on either side of the door. Alice was astonished to see the captain of one of the ships enter. He must have had an interesting journey from his ship to the Blazing Blunderbuss, as the only thing connecting the two ships was a rope, and the wind was still whipping outside.

His crew obviously respected him, as the soldiers all stood a little straighter when he entered.

Hara greeted the captain first. "Welcome to the Blazing Blunderbuss. I'm Captain Hara and this is my crew. We're glad we found you after that storm."

The captain raised an eyebrow. He undoubtedly suspected the reason they were this far south was because they had been avoiding the Empress rather than answering her summons. He was polite enough not to bring it up. Alice wondered if subtle manipulation of the situation was something Hara had learned from her father.

Hara's father had used Hara's engineering abilities to further his cons. Alice wouldn't bring it up with Hara as she would see it as something abhorrent, but Alice believed it was prudent for Hara to use the skills she had learned at her father's knee.

"It's indeed lucky, Captain Hara. I'm Captain Bai. We were searching for you to offer an escort when the storm blew us off course. The Empress smiles on us indeed." The captain crouched down to speak with the foo-lion.

He spoke in Chinese but Shilong whispered in Alice's ear the translation. "You've delivered your message. You can return to your own kind now."

The foo-lion remained still. Angel chittered and Captain Bai studied her for a long moment. He straightened. "It seems you have gained the loyalty of Shishi."

Hara raised an eyebrow. "Shishi? Is that his name? He's certainly taken a liking to Angel."

Captain Bai watched the two clockwork creatures. "You don't consider her your belonging?"

"She's in my collection but she's her own being," Hara answered without hesitation. Hara was comfortable with the idea of collections. Maybe Shilong had been right; that humans had picked up more than Alice realised from the dragons.

"I see," said Captain Bai in a clipped tone, though Alice wasn't sure what he thought of the defection of the metal creature.

In Han, all the positions of power were held by the dragons, and Captain Bai was clearly human. Alice wasn't surprised he would know the difference between being owned and being in a collection in an attempt to survive among dragons.

His eyes rested on Shilong. He frowned. "I didn't expect to see you here."

Shilong shrugged. "My work takes me to interesting places." Captain Bai continued to frown but eventually bowed his head slowly to Shilong and turned back to Hara.

Captain Bai motioned to one of his men and said to Hara, "I'll leave one of my signal men with you to help expedite your travel into Han."

Everyone knew he was there to make sure they actually followed them into Han. The Blazing Blunderbuss could never outrun the power that was in the military airships, no matter how fast she was.

Hara smiled but it didn't reach her eyes. "Thank you, Captain Bai."

With that he nodded his head and his contingent, minus the signal man, left. Hara watched the empty doorway for a long moment. The signalman politely went over to the windows at the front of the bridge.

He was far enough away that when Hara spoke softly he didn't hear. "We could run."

Shilong said, "I would not advise you to run. The Jade Empress rules with an iron fist. The last man to ignore her summons was hunted down across two continents and brought to her on his knees. They firebombed his ship. To defy the Empress is a dangerous undertaking. Others have tried and all have regretted it."

Hara said more to herself than to the crew, "It looks like we're going to Han after all." She turned to Shilong. "Your trip with us will be shorter than expected."

Alice hadn't factored that in and her heart flopped sideways in her chest. She wasn't ready to see him leave. She doubted she ever would be.

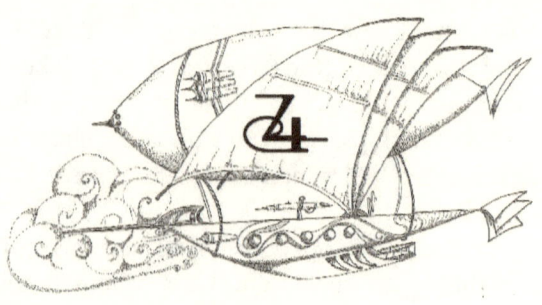

Hara leaned on the railing that bordered the bridge. Gideon ordinarily sat up here and watched the world disappear beneath him. Hara wondered if their child would take up the same habit. She propped her head up on her hand.

She deliberately shied away from the thought of her child, so she prodded the feeling to figure out why she wasn't so keen. She thought she had accepted the whole deal when it came to Gideon—a relationship and children and everything else that came with being bonded to a dragon.

Hara imagined the child on her lap. Golden eyes like its father. No, it wasn't the child that bothered her, it was something else. It had to be something that had happened between accepting Gideon and now.

A wound opened up. Gideon. Gideon had always been open with her; honest to a fault at times. He never did things sneakily. That was what her father did: lie and hide the truth in order to manipulate people.

Hara looked up when Gideon approached her. She could see he was cautious as he leaned on the railing next to her. He said, looking down at the ground beneath them, "This country has some interesting views. Mountains like you can't find anywhere else in the world. There are some fantastic caves down there. There's one cave discovered by a monk escaping the Jade Dragon Empress and her soldiers. He called it Stone Flower."

He pointed to the ground where they could barely see the worn path where people travelled to get to the cave. "This area is dotted with dozens of caves. My favorite is the Shihua caves. That is where the monk lived. When the dragons decided to take over Han, some refugees found their way to these hills and they met the monk. One man had a basket with some children in it who had run away from the dragon armies. When the monk looked into the basket, he didn't see human children; instead he saw two baby dragons. The refugees realised then that the dragon empire was here to stay. I doubt they were really baby dragons as there have been no baby dragons born in Han." His voice was sad at the end.

Hara let him talk as she needed to gather her courage, but now she was sure of what she wanted to say, so she interrupted before he could continue with his babbling. "You lied to me. Not with words, but with silence, and it feels just like a lie."

Gideon frowned. "I didn't know silence could lie."

Anger and frustration warred inside of Hara and she confronted Gideon. "Don't avoid this conversation, Gideon, you owe me that at least. You manipulated me. You knew I didn't know much about babies and dragons and how all that stuff works. You made me think having a child was a vague possibility. You, on the other hand, knew exactly what was happening, and you used my ignorance to bulldoze over the top of me. If you had been honest and talked with me about having kids, then I wouldn't be so mad at you."

Gideon looked sheepish. "You would've argued."

"Yes, because I have valid reasons for putting off children. Like the fact we live on an ex-pirate ship.

Couldn't you have waited until our reputation for being pirates was just a memory? Now I have to worry about being attacked by pretty much everyone and a child at the same time. Also, I like to think things over. I don't like to be rushed into things before I've had time to mull over it all. So, I'd have appreciated the time to think."

"You can think now," Gideon added helpfully.

Hara shook her head. "Not the same and you know it." She pointed a finger at him. "You lie to me again with silence or words and I'll throw you off this ship, and for good this time."

Hara spun on her heels and left Gideon standing at the front of the bridge. She had forgotten they hadn't been alone. The others looked at the ground and determinedly not at either of them. Sighing in frustration, Hara decided to find another place where she could truly be private.

<hr/>

Yeijing city was massive, and the jewel in the crown of the dragon Han empire. They had built it to show the power and majesty of their reign. Alice had been impressed by Versailles, but Yeijing dwarfed it as the Blazing Blunderbuss followed Captain Bai's ship. The city had areas crammed with buildings that leaned together like drunken sailors on shore leave. There were also towering temples with roofs twisted up at the corners to point to heaven, and massive expanses of gardens and rounded walls.

Alice said, "Those watch towers are pointing the wrong way. They look towards the palace, not out over the city."

Shilong said, "They're watching for when the Empress rises to mate. You see, when a dragon is ready to mate, she will fly straight up into the sky and give out a call that can be heard for a long distance. Those towers are there for all the male dragons of the Han. They're waiting for the promised day when the Empress will choose her Emperor."

Alice twisted her head to get a better look at the towers. The windows were indeed large enough for a dragon to change and jump out of.

Curious, Alice asked, "How many times has she flown to mate?"

"Never. To choose a mate would diminish her power."

Alice snapped her head around to look at Shilong. "That can't be right. There are only a handful of female dragons in this world." Alice had only ever heard of one female dragon, and that was the Jade Empress. She didn't know of any other female dragons on the whole planet.

"Four, as far as we know, though it's thought one died in the new world years ago as we haven't heard from her," he said.

"Surely the continuation of your race is more important than sharing power?" Alice could not even imagine four women left on a planet with thousands of males.

"Not according to the Empress. She took over the Han with the support of the male dragons in the area, who helped her, hoping they would impress her and she'd choose one of them to mate with. But it's been a thousand years since she took the throne and she hasn't left the palace since it was built."

"What do the other dragons think? Can't they force her to fly? I mean, well, doesn't she want to mate with any of the dragons?" Alice could hardly believe she had even for a moment contemplated forcing a woman to do something as important as choosing a mate.

"You have to be aware of the dragon culture. The women ruled there. There were always more males than there were females. When the females flew, they'd stay out of reach until the male they wanted was the only one flying, then they would surrender. Here on this planet the Empress has hundreds of males to choose from. But while they all think they've a chance to mate with her they'll be loyal. The moment she chooses one, the others will find other mates and their loyalty will no longer be with the Empress."

"That's sick and twisted," said Alice. For a thousand years the Empress had led on all those dragons with something she obviously was never going to surrender. She could at least have given them leave to find others.

"It's lucky Captain Bai is escorting your captain, as the Empress has forbidden other dragons to mate with humans," said Shilong. "Hara should perhaps cover up her branding marks as some might not realise she was summoned and throw her into prison."

"What? That's barbaric. To not let the others marry either. Not even humans." Alice shook her head at the thought. She wondered if Hara was aware. She was getting ready for her audience with the Empress.

The Blazing Blunderbuss was given a berth next to other military airships. It was almost on the other side of the city from the summer palace, and it would be a trek for Hara to get to the gardens that surrounded the palace. Alice assumed they had docked so far away because the Empress didn't trust either her military or Hara.

⬥━━━━━━━━━━━━━━━━━━━━━⬥

Hara wore the gown Captain Bai had sent over. It was worse than the gown she had had to wear to see the Emperor of the Wyvern Empire. The gown was made of silk in a bright blue with gold thread.

It sheathed her legs with screeds of cloth so she wouldn't be able to run even if she pulled up the skirts. The sleeves were ridiculous, draping off her arms like bulky wings, but there was no sign of a corset at least. If only she could fly, as the skirt was so elaborate she could only take shuffling steps. The top was even worse as the collar jabbed at the bottom of her chin and threatened to strangle her.

Shilong knocked on the door just as she was about to throw the whole dress out the window and helped her.

Gideon said from the bed, "You look beautiful." He had finished dressing ages ago and had watched with fascination as Shilong brushed out Hara's hair and pinned it to her head.

Hara winced as Shilong put in the final pin. Her hair felt like it would pull her face off if she smiled. "Are you still trying to flatter me?"

"Yes, is it working?"

Hara smiled while her back was facing Gideon, so he wouldn't see her expression. Shilong raised an eyebrow but made no comment.

Hara said, "Maybe. I want some more grovelling though."

"As you wish, my dear," Gideon said obsequiously.

Hara asked Shilong, "Anything you can tell us about the Empress?"

"She's a she-dragon," he said succinctly.

Hara rolled her eyes. "Something more useful than that."

Gideon said, "That's useful. She-dragons are particular. They want to collect the world. On our planet men weren't allowed to have collections. Only here have we been able to make our own collections. Female dragons are ambitious and vicious. They also see

37

collections differently to men. They take them for granted. We've been denied for so long that we appreciate our collections, but not she-dragons."

"She does not consider the humans to be in her collection," Shilong explained.

Gideon sat up straighter on the bed. "Really? That's interesting. What does she see them as?"

"They are subjects. They are there to serve her. The male dragons have not realised yet, but they are not in her collection either. She tells them lies and placates them." Shilong's green eyes sparked with secrets held.

"Is there a rebellion?" Gideon was clearly interested in this conversation.

"Yes," Shilong answered succinctly.

Hara asked, "Will that make things difficult for us while we're here?" The political issues weren't really her problem. They would talk to the Empress and then they would leave. That was the advantage of living on an airship.

Shilong shrugged but gave his best opinion. "It's most likely why the Empress has called you." He nodded at Gideon. "Some will assume she has asked you here to mate with, as you are brother to an emperor."

Gideon grunted. "I have a mate, thank you very much."

Hara said dryly, "Not for long if you annoy me too much."

"Nonsense. I drove you up the wall while I was courting you and you didn't even kick me off the ship."

"Reminding me while I'm still angry with you is not the best thing right now, Gideon, and besides, I distinctly remember leaving you back in the middle of the Wyvern Empire. You snuck back onto the airship. Into my bed, to be factual."

A scratching noise came from the door. Shilong went to answer it and the foo-lion, Shishi, entered with Angel riding on his back.

Hara bent over at the waist to address the small dragon. "You're going to get lazy if you keep riding him like that."

Shilong said, "I've never seen one of the Empress's foo-lions act like this."

Hara said with a laugh in her voice, "You've seen many of the foo-lions, then?"

Gideon answered, "He should've. He's a dragon."

Hara turned to Gideon. "What? Why didn't you tell me?" She turned back to Shilong. "Does Alice know?"

Gideon asked, "Why would it matter what Alice knows?"

Hara ignored him and kept her gaze on Shilong.

"I'm not sure," Shilong said honestly. It was clear that he didn't see the issue that Hara did.

"I can tell you she'll be madder than a knocked-over nest of bees when you tell her. If you thought I was mad at Gideon for not telling me I could easily get pregnant, then just think what she'll be like. Her first love betrayed her by pretending to be in love with her just to get her into bed, and when she refused to sleep with him, he spread rumours about her."

"I wouldn't do that." Shilong frowned in mild confusion and offense as he spoke.

Hara threw up her hands in frustration. "Men. You don't understand. It's the deception she'll react to. She'll lump you in the same category as her cad of a beau."

Shilong frowned. Hara was glad she was getting through to him.

She said, "If you mate with her, I suggest you make it extremely clear what it entails. Mating between humans

39

is very different to what happens between humans and dragons."

Shilong said, confused, "Our anatomy is the same."

Hara looked up at the roof and muttered a short prayer for patience. "I'm not talking about how your bodies will fit together. I'm talking about cultural differences. Women in our culture will mate once with a male and it will be enjoyable but it won't be a declaration of love."

"You can mate and not love at the same time?" The revelation shocked Shilong.

"Yes. Look at Susan and Murphy. They'll not mate forever."

Shilong admitted, "I don't understand this."

Hara patted him on his shoulder. "Well, if you want to mate with a human you'll have to learn. We can choose who we love and it's important to us to have the right to choose who our mates are."

Gideon said, "It's forbidden."

Hara turned to Gideon. "What?"

Gideon explained. "The Empress has forbidden any dragon in her collection to mate with a human. She arrests both and puts them in prison indefinitely until the woman breaks the bond."

"Wait, we can get divorced?" Hara asked, amazed, though she knew she would have no need for the information as she and Gideon were in it for the long haul.

"Yes, but only the woman can divorce the male. Remember, we're a matriarchal society back on our planet. There are still dragons in prison because they mated with women. The women have long since died of old age. I wouldn't have brought you here if I didn't think we could play the card that we are both in another

40

collection—one that doesn't belong to the Empress. Also, it helps that Captain Bai was kind enough to send over clothes that hide both of our bonding marks." He preened over his silk outfit like a seasoned dandy and flicked an imaginary bit of fluff off one sleeve.

Hara flapped her sleeves in frustration. "That's ridiculous. She's only hurting her own kind by doing that. Well, let us see this Empress and then get out of here. I like the architecture but I think I'm already sick with the injustices."

Gideon got off the bed and turned her around. "We might have to do what she asks, for political reasons. That might mean staying longer than you wish." Gideon didn't always like to admit that his brother was the father of the Wyvern Empire. It had its advantages and disadvantages even at the best of times.

"I know. It doesn't mean I have to like it." Hara's voice had a sharp snap to it that wasn't directed at Gideon.

Shilong said, "Your track record is causing mayhem rather than going along with things as planned."

Hara grinned and looked at Shilong. "You're right, Shilong. The Empress might regret summoning us."

"I'm counting on it."

Hara patted Shilong's shoulder as she passed him to leave the room. "You fit well here, Shilong. Let us hope Alice doesn't cut off something important when she finds out you're a dragon."

Shilong turned to Gideon. "Does she know what she has just offered?"

"Yes. She would be happy to have you in her collection." There was a smile in Gideon's voice.

Shilong shook his head. "I've never been in someone's collection before, not really," he said the last wistfully. Hara wasn't surprised he didn't count the Empress, even though he was a Han dragon.

Gideon patted his shoulder and grinned at him. "It's by far the most amazing thing if it's with the right person." With that comment Gideon followed Hara out of the room and off the Blazing Blunderbuss.

Captain Bai waited for them while they descended on the lift. There was no way Hara would be able to climb a ladder in a dress, even one with a bit less material than the one she was wearing, though she did wonder how Alice managed to do it all the time. She had tried to get Alice to wear breeches but the woman liked dresses. Especially ones with pockets.

Hara asked Gideon, "Do you think the Empress makes women wear these to stop them from running away? Or suffocating them if they actually do try to run?" She tugged at the collar of the tunic.

Gideon answered, "I don't think the Empress even wears clothes."

"What?" Surely Hara had heard wrong.

"The Empress only stays as a dragon. I don't think anyone has seen her human form in almost a thousand years." Hara supposed that made sense. The Empress was in her own domain and there was no reason for her to play nice with the humans. Hara doubted humans had seen much of her either, even in dragon form.

Captain Bai said, "I have organised a tram for our use."

Hara said, "In other words, you kicked off a whole lot of civilians so we could ride in it." Captain Bai wisely did not respond to Hara's retort.

Gideon said, "You're a bit sharp today."

"Blame it on my pregnancy," she said this softly to Gideon so only he could hear.

Captain Bai tried for some conversation. "Did you know Han doctors are some of the best in the world? They might have some potions to help you with your mood."

"I assure you women know all of them."

Gideon said, "Men know them as well. Trust me."

Hara hit him on his arm and he just grinned at her. He said after a while, "Forgive me yet?"

"Not until after I've had the baby and you're looking after it."

Captain Bai was brave as he asked, "Are you about to be a mother, Captain Hara?"

"Yes. Though it was a little unexpected," Hara admitted.

Captain Bai frowned. "How can a pregnancy be unexpected?" Which proved to Hara that he didn't have a significant other.

Gideon chortled and Hara glared at him. She turned back to the captain. "I was unaware dragons were so fertile with humans. That is how it was unexpected."

The captain went pale, which said a lot as he was already a pale man. He coughed to hide his reaction. "You're mated to a dragon?"

Hara remembered it was forbidden. "The Empress is aware. She called me a child bride. I suppose from her perspective I am a child." The Empress's mistake, as far as Hara was concerned. Gideon had always treated Hara with respect for her mind and enjoyed watching her as she decimated whole armies with only her wit. It was a mistake for the Empress to underestimate her.

Hara glanced over at Gideon, and she realised his amusement was over what she would do. The sharpness in her caused by the pregnancy only upped the stakes as far as he was concerned. He had once told her one of the things he loved about her was that she could make people change even if they didn't want to.

Hara shook her head slightly and turned back to the captain. "In the Wyvern Empire many of the nobility are married to dragons. It's a common practise there."

This new information shocked the captain. "It's allowed? I thought the abominations of the union were non-viable. Why would a noble woman want to mate with a dragon if all their children were monsters?"

Gideon chuckled, and Hara could imagine he was thinking of his brother's children. One of them had been William the Conqueror, and to some he might have been considered a monster.

"I think you're mistaken, Captain. Children of those unions are very much like dragons. If you consider dragons as monsters, then I suppose you aren't wrong."

Gideon showed some teeth, which wasn't nearly as impressive as when he was a dragon. "Nom nom."

In Han there was no such treaty of non-aggression between humans and dragons. The humans had lost the war here and they were subject to dragons and their whims, though from Hara's understanding the dragons in Han did not eat humans as a given rule, even though there was nothing to stop them.

The tram ride allowed them to take in the view of Yeijing in a casual way. The tram dropped them at the edge of the extensive gardens that surrounded the summer palace.

Captain Bai stopped at the gates where several foo-lions came out to greet them.

Gideon said, "They're all male."

The captain frowned. "Excuse me?"

Gideon pointed to the foo-lions. "All the clockwork creatures are male."

"You'd give a gender to a machine?" Captain Bai looked at Gideon rather than at the foo-lions.

"These have identities. Gender is part of that. So of course, I'd acknowledge that. Whoever made them made them all male," Gideon explained kindly.

The captain shrugged. "Around the temples there are female and male foo-lions, but these creatures were made for the Empress and they are all alike. I suppose it's to represent all the dragons that protect her as these do."

Hara bent to look at one closer. It tilted up its head to study her. Hara said softly, "Cruel."

Gideon asked, "Why do you say that?"

"To make them forever alone, and also always the same as others."

Gideon said sagely, "Yes, that is cruel."

Hara looked at him. He would know better than anyone. Most of the dragons who had come to this planet had been male. Gideon, unlike the other dragons, had immersed himself in human culture. He would understand what it meant to be alone while in a crowd. To be the same but always completely different.

Hara turned back to the foo-lions. "Shishi has made a friend."

She motioned to Shishi and Angel. Angel chittered in greeting. The foo-lions turned to study Angel. Hara wasn't sure what they thought of it all. Shishi wasn't demonstrative and his fellow foo-lions weren't either.

Hara carried on. "He might want to come with us later. That's his choice. I bring this up now as you will need to decide if you will allow him."

The captain said, "The foo-lions belong to the Empress."

Hara didn't straighten out of her crouch but turned her head to look at Captain Bai. "Are they in her

45

collection? She doesn't even consider you to be in her collection, so why would she think they are? Besides, it's always the choice of the collected to decide whether to be part of the collection or not."

Hara turned back to the foo lions "I'll treat him with respect and maintain him. He'll be allowed any upgrades he wishes and I'll keep him in parts."

Gideon placed a hand to his heart and batted his eyelashes, pretending to be teary-eyed. "You're going to be a great mother."

Hara straightened up. "Don't start with me, Gideon."

Hara turned to the captain. "We're ready."

The captain shifted his feet nervously. "No humans are allowed past the foo-lions."

Hara raised an eyebrow. The Empress sounded like an interesting character, but also a lonely one. "I hope, Captain Bai, this is not goodbye."

Captain Bai bowed his head slightly to her, acknowledging her words. He turned sharply on his heels and headed back to his ship.

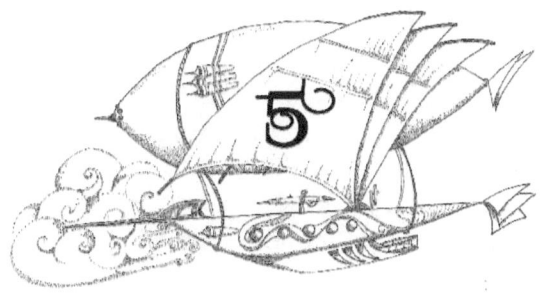

Looking at the gates of the palace, Hara said to Gideon, "You're to make sure she doesn't eat me."

She stepped into the crowd of foo-lions with Shishi and Angel at her side. The foo-lions shifted to make a formation around them.

Gideon said, "You do know that female dragons are almost twice the size of male dragons?"

"But you're smarter," Hara retorted.

He smirked, proud of his mate's comment. "I might be, but she's conniving. All female dragons are."

"Don't worry about that. Just make sure she doesn't eat me." Hara turned to Angel. "The Empress will not like that you've made friends with Shishi. Despite the fact she doesn't want to keep him in her collection, she won't want others to collect him. So you need to hide that you've added him to your collection."

Angel chittered, then opened her wings and hopped up to Hara's arm, crawling up to her shoulder. Hara reached up and stroked her nose.

The troop of foo-lions led them past small lakes and through stunning gardens until they reached a small boat. Hara assumed they were to ride in the boat. It certainly wasn't big enough for all the foo-lions. The Empress wasn't interested in seeing them either, it seemed.

Hara said to Shishi, "You and Angel can wait here." It would be safer if Angel wasn't with them. She chittered in protest. Shishi made a waffling sound and Angel settled down. She glided off Hara's shoulder and landed on Shishi again.

Hara said, "You take care of her."

Shishi remained motionless. Hara really would have to talk to him about showing his thought process somehow. Angel had never had trouble showing what she was thinking or feeling.

Hara and Gideon boarded the boat and she said, "I wish I could stay back with Angel."

"The Empress won't eat you," Gideon assured her. He clearly knew where her true concern was.

"She might. She sounds vicious."

"Only if you provoke her." He looked at her for a long moment then smiled. "Sorry, I forgot who I was talking to."

Hara wrinkled her nose at his light teasing. She could play it cool, but she wondered if a female dragon might deal better with someone who acted like another female dragon. Gideon picked up the punt and moved their boat out onto the lake.

He said, "I could always do the talking. She did summon me. Not like last time when the Emperor only wanted to talk to you. I felt like a third wheel."

"Jealous?" His indignant tone amused her.

"Yes. Of course. I'm gorgeous, people should always pay attention to me first." Hara smiled and then covered the emotion.

Gideon said, "Ah, I think you've forgiven me."

Hara didn't dignify that with an answer.

Strangely enough, it was easier to approach the dragon Empress than it had been to visit with the

Emperor of the Wyvern Empire. Hara thought it had something to do with growing up in the shadow of the Emperor that intimidated her. She had only heard about the Empress while they had travelled. In this part of the world, she was the shadow that kept people awake at night.

They came to a small jetty and Hara held the edge as she climbed out of the boat. The excessive fabric threatened to topple her but she caught herself at the last moment. They were on an island in the middle of a lake. There was a delicate building with enormous gates for them to enter. There were jewels encrusted in the walls of an open-air courtyard.

Hara hadn't realised she was looking at the dragon Empress until the wall moved. What had seemed like emeralds were actually scales.

Hara whispered to Gideon, "I thought dragons were all gold."

Both Gideon and Harlen were gold dragons. Hara wondered if that was just a family thing now that she was looking at a dragon that was clearly another colour.

"That's more regional. The Wyvern Empire dragons are gold. A lesser dragon on our planet, but I think we've done well for ourselves. The dragons who came to this area of the world are mostly green, white or pearl in colour."

A voice boomed, "Enter."

Hara shot a sharp glance at Gideon. She hadn't realised that female dragons could speak. Gideon wasn't verbal when he was a dragon. He sounded more like Angel when he was in dragon form and she didn't understand anything he said. The Jade Empress not only spoke discernible language, she spoke in a language Hara could understand. Obviously, the Empress had been anticipating them.

Hara shuffled forward. The gates opened up into a massive courtyard where the Jade Empress was curled on highly decorated floors. Hara had seen dragons before and they were as large as a small cottage. The Empress was bigger, but not mansion-sized. Her head was twice as large as Gideon's, and maybe he had been right to worry that he couldn't stop her from eating anyone she wanted. The Empress's head was propped up on one of her arms, which was tucked under her chin.

She huffed out some hot air. "So you're the lost prince and his child bride."

Gideon said, "I wasn't aware that I was lost, Radiant Highness."

"Ha, very funny. You disappeared for centuries." She waved dismissively with one of her claws. The human gesture looked strange on the large creature.

"That was on purpose. So technically, not lost."

She clicked a claw on the stone floor to dismiss his words. "You're a prince, though."

"Again, technically not that either. My brother was the father of an Emperor. That's as close as I come to royalty, and as the great Jade Empress is aware, merely being related to someone does not make them royalty. I was never in my brother's or my nephew's collections."

The Empress complained, "You're trying my patience, dragon. Change to your true form and we can have a proper conversation."

This was when Hara stepped forward. "Not so fast, Radiant Highness. We come as a pair, so if anyone wants our help they would have to deal with us as a pair."

The Empress growled and slammed a claw right next to Hara. Gideon transformed in an instant and with a growl got between Hara and the Empress.

Gideon wrapped his tail around Hara's waist and placed her on his back. Hara ran up his spine to his head. Holding one of the ridges on his head she said, "We can leave, Empress, or you can talk to us."

The Empress growled. She wasn't pleased with the rude breach of etiquette. Hara didn't care. The Empress had basically shanghaied them to come and visit her, and she would deal with them fairly or they would leave, even if it meant fighting their way out.

The Empress blew out hot air that pinkened Hara's skin, then backed off. She waved an indifferent claw. "Fine."

Gideon shuffled back and Hara hopped down from his neck. Hara said, "Then, Radiant Highness, why has the Han Empire asked for our attendance here in this wonderful palace?"

The Empress moved around the sizable floor and picked up random things as she spoke. "Someone tried to poison me. They killed one of my loyal servants."

Hara's heart dropped. They had been so sure they had prevented the release of the poison that had been designed by a crazy Roshian professor. Her father had been intending to deliver the professor and his poison that killed bonded dragons to the Roshians, who happened to hate all dragons. Hara had managed to intervene and now the professor was cooking up other things in a secret laboratory in the heart of the Wyvern Empire where he would cause no problems. She had no idea how some of the poison had reached Han, but it wasn't a good sign.

The Empress put down what she had and moved to a fountain and dipped her claws. Hara wasn't fooled. The Empress was not distracted in the least. If she wanted to be a bit rude to get back at them Hara would overlook it.

"I suspect it's rampion."

Hara had thought that was a made-up plant, but Gideon, still in his dragon form, curled his tail around Hara. The Empress continued, "We had some rebels in our prisons so we questioned them but they had no answers. There are rebels still out in our land. Most of them wouldn't have been able to bring the rampion here from our home world."

Ah, now Hara understood. When the dragons came over from their own planet they had not been able to bring a lot. It would have taken a lot of concentration and calculations to bring over anything at all. If rampion was a herb from their planet it would also have been hard to come by, as shortly before the dragons had come over their planet had been turned into a fire ball and all the plants had been burned to a crisp.

Gideon, as one of the mathematicians who had been part of the project to come over to Earth, would know what calculations would have been needed. He was really the best person to seek out someone who had a poison from their home world. It seemed they were staying after all.

Hara said, "If we find this traitor, Radiant Highness, then we would want to deal with them, without interference from the Han soldiers or the imperial guard." She had heard horror stories of how the Han dealt with their prisoners, and she would never let someone be tortured, even if they were a traitor. The crew were in this part of the world just because they would rather exile a dragon than have him killed or tortured.

The Empress flicked her tail impatiently. "You bargain everything to death. Fine, you'll have freedom to deal with this traitor as you see fit. Just find them."

Hara was sure there was more to the story than just the poison attempt, but it was unlikely the Empress would tell them or that she even knew the whole story. Hara motioned to Gideon. He picked her up again and placed her on his back.

Hara waited for the formal dismissal. Though it was clear the conversation was over, the Empress waited just a little longer than was appropriate before she flicked a claw in dismissal.

Hara leaned forward on Gideon's back. "Let's pick up the children before we leave." Hara wasn't going to mention that one of the children she spoke of was the Empress's foo-lion. The Empress could pretend the foo-lion stayed with Hara and Gideon on her own orders— unless Hara forced her to make a declaration.

<hr>

Captain Bai wasn't waiting for Hara and Gideon when they left the palace. Since they had travelled on the tram it was easy enough to find their way back to the military port where the Blazing Blunderbuss was harboured.

Hara looked up at the sky and the roofline. There was a creature on one of the roofs of the buildings. It was hard to discern as there were many strange protrusions from the buildings, but Hara was watching when it moved. She grabbed Gideon's arm and pointed. He glanced up just as the thing jumped off the roof.

Wings snapped out and it flew off.

Hara asked, "Did that thing have a monkey's tail?"

"That's Sun Wukong."

Hara glanced at Gideon. He had travelled a lot in his life and hadn't only stayed in the Wyvern Empire. He had already demonstrated that he knew the Han Empire very well.

He motioned with his head to indicate the black dot that was the flying monkey thing. "Sun Wukong is a fairy tale they tell children. Wukong was first a stone monkey who was king of the monkeys. One day he realised he would die and he didn't like that idea. So he took on the gods themselves to be as immortal as they are."

Hara pointed in the direction of the strange creature. "That wasn't a fairy tale. That's real."

Gideon shrugged. "If I was a human and lived here, I might use the legends to get a bit of notoriety for my cause."

Hara looked where the black dot had now disappeared. She wondered if they had walked into the middle of a political storm. Gideon knew how to wade through those waters, but Hara knew someone who could swim the waters and come out fighting. It might be time to call for some help.

***

Charani chased chickens around with her cousin. Lala watched nervously. Lala might have been born among the Romani but she wasn't one of them. She was a dragon hunter and so was Charani. The child, though, was also part Romani, and so had a place here that Lala never would.

Harlen said from the step of the wagon he sat on, "She'll be fine."

"She's still mine." There was doubt in Lala's voice. Lala had found Charani when she was only two years old in a caravan that had been raided by bandits. The bandits had left Charani to die in the harsh elements. It had only been luck that Lala's dragon hunter abilities had warned her there had been another of her kind nearby. Lala had almost ignored them. Dragon hunters in groups tended to die young.

That was what had happened to her parents. They had tried to make a dragon hunter community. The locals had been worried that it would draw the attention of dragons their way, so they had taken out the small community one night. Lala had escaped because she had been out hunting and had gotten stuck in a sink hole overnight. She had been sixteen and she had been alone since then. Until Charani and until Harlen.

She looked over at Harlen, who looked too casual. Harlen was never casual. They hadn't known each other long but that was something she was learning about him.

He glanced at her. "What?"

"You're keeping something from me."

He raised an eyebrow. "Is that women's intuition, or is that something the dragon hunter part of you is saying?"

"That wasn't a no." She avoided the question as she wasn't sure of the answer. She wasn't comfortable with the dragon hunter abilities, though Harlen constantly encouraged her to use them.

He hesitated then said, "Hara asked for us to go to Han. I don't like Han."

Lala wasn't fooled. She motioned to where Charani played. "Is that why we've come to visit Charani's grandparents?"

Harlen tilted his head sideways a little. It was moments like this that reminded her he was more animal than human. "I suppose so. I still don't like Han."

"Why? Isn't there a dragon in charge? I would've thought you would've liked that."

"This isn't our world. We might be superior beings but that doesn't mean that we've the right to rule."

Lala snorted at that sentiment. She had met Harlen's brother. He might not officially be the Emperor but he ruled the Wyvern Empire regardless. For Harlen to object to what was happening in Han meant it wasn't just about ruling a human country, it was something else.

She waited for him to elaborate. He usually became antsy if she tried to get it out of him when he wasn't ready.

Charani came up to Lala and tugged on her shirt. "Lala. Lala. Did you hear? My grandparents want me to stay a while. Can I? Can I? Can I?"

By the repetition Lala knew Charani was serious. Charani had grown up rapidly so was typically a serious girl despite her young age.

Lala stooped down. "You'll have to promise to listen to your grandparents even when you think they're being silly. If you can't promise that then I won't be able to trust you to stay here."

"What if they ask me to kill a dragon? I don't think I can kill dragons anymore." Like the four-year-old had ever killed a dragon. Charani had taken to Harlen instantly. Lala wasn't sure why, as he was a brusque man even with Charani, but he always made sure she was looked after. Lala wondered if Charani's idea of kindness was skewed because she had been with Lala too long.

Lala raised an eyebrow and Charani sighed. "Okay, I promise I'll listen to Granpa and Granma."

"By listen, you mean do everything they say." Lala didn't want Charani to weasel out of obeying her grandparents on a technicality.

"Yes." Though Charani said this slowly and reluctantly.

"Then yes, you can stay with your grandparents. Harlen and I are going to Han, so you won't be able to change your mind."

"Han? I want to go. Can I go?" Lala shook her head. If Harlen had set up visiting the Romani so conveniently, he must have had some idea of what they were heading into. And judging by the stories Lala had heard of Hara, she could imagine it would be trouble. Charani frowned but got over her disappointment swiftly and ran off to continue chasing her cousin who had caught the chicken.

Harlen said, "We should leave soon. Hara isn't one to blow things out of proportion."

Curious, Lala asked, "What did she say?"

"Just that there was trouble in Han."

"You do know that Han isn't in your collection? You don't have to make sure it's looked after."

Harlen got up from the step. "If the Han destabilise then they will harbour villains who will prey on my people."

"That's a little convoluted," Lala said with a small frown as she sorted the details out in her head. His logic most days confused her.

"I don't need an excuse. Hara asked for help."

"She isn't in your collection either." Lala was only starting to understand what collections meant. At first she had thought, like many others, that it was a form of slavery. Apparently, it was something much more complicated, and she still hadn't gotten a satisfactory answer out of her stoic mate.

Harlen grumbled. "Dragons don't have much in the way of family. Just our mates. I like the concept of family.

It's why I work for my brother. Hara…Hara is family. Maybe not in my collection, but family."

Lala almost laughed. He cared about Hara and wanted to help but wasn't sure why. He had this idea of family but she wasn't sure he understood it completely.

Lala asked, "Will the Empress mind us just popping in?"

"Most likely, but she hasn't been looking after her collection. It was only a matter of time before those outside of her collection started stealing it." He didn't act concerned about making trouble.

"I thought you were trying to avoid destabilisation." Lala did enjoy pointing out to him when he had flawed logic.

"The greater good does not justify mistreating your collection."

It was Harlen's strong views on how a collection should be treated that had convinced Lala to marry him. She didn't love him yet, but from what she had seen of him so far she did think it was possible. Others had married for less, and she knew anyone who cared for Charani was worth it. Besides, attraction had never been a problem, so it was hardly a sacrifice.

As they left the camp, she said to Harlen, "This isn't the only thing that's worrying you."

He was silent for a long moment, then said, "We've been mated for two months now."

Lala raised an eyebrow but didn't say anything. She wanted to see where he would go with this.

He was quiet for a long moment then asked, "Is our love-making not adequate?"

Lala coughed her astonishment at the question. She had forgotten he liked bluntness, and she had invited him to air his issues with her. She rubbed the back of her neck then said, "No, it's more than adequate." She blushed profusely. She wasn't used to talking about her sex life. Not that she had had one before meeting Harlen.

She felt she had to add more. "I didn't expect I'd marry anyone before I met you, Harlen. I mean, I was dragging around someone else's kid. Most men wouldn't even take on a woman with a kid from another marriage, let alone what they would consider a stray. Then add in that I have dragon hunter blood and the risks that involves. I really didn't think wedding bells were in my future at all."

Not that there had been any wedding bells in their mating.

Lala had been living in an abandoned warehouse when Harlen had found her and Charani. They had been starving and trapped in a small town in the Middle East with no clear way to get out of the situation. Lala had been contemplating selling her body for food when he had rescued them.

She had put up a fight as she was fiercely independent, but she also wasn't stupid. He didn't fear her dragon hunter blood. He was good to Charani and applauded Lala for taking her in. Harlen was a good man and he wanted her—more than she wanted him, but even that didn't seem to bother him too much. Or so she had thought.

Lala sighed. "Is it because I haven't said the L word yet?"

Harlen groused. "It isn't the word that I need."

He didn't add more and Lala wanted to swear in frustration at his penny pinching ways when it came to words. She asked instead, "What do you want from me, then?"

He was quiet for longer than she expected. "I want you to be emotionally invested in our relationship."

Lala raised an eyebrow. "Isn't that the same thing?"

Harlen simply said, "No."

Lala decided she would leave the conversation there. She had some thinking to do. It wasn't that she didn't care for Harlen. She could always say the words. That was when she realised what he meant; that it wasn't the same. He didn't want the words. He wanted the feeling.

Alice looked up when Captain Bai arrived on the bridge. He was alone and he looked a little lost without his soldiers with him. Alice asked, "Is there something we can help you with, Captain Bai?"

He had taken off his hat and had it in both of his hands. He twisted it around nervously. "I've been told to make sure all your needs are seen to, and I thought I'd invite you to a Cuju game. Everyone, that is. I mean, you're all invited."

Alice smiled at his nervous manner. He had seemed much more sure of himself when he was dealing with orders that he understood. Hara had told her he had been a little discombobulated by her mating with Gideon, and by the discovery that she was pregnant. From what Shilong had told Alice about the Han, she wasn't astonished that he was upset at the blasé way they treated the laws.

Alice said, "I'm sure some of us would love to get off the ship for a bit. None of us have been out much except for Hara and Gideon, who have been looking for assassins."

Captain Bai didn't act shocked by her revelation that there were assassins wandering around Yeijing. Either he knew something the crew didn't, or he didn't think they were a danger to him. Alice went to the speaker to call down to the engine room.

When Angel came up with the foo-lion Alice hunkered down to speak to the mechanical dragon. "Captain Bai here has invited us on an outing. Can you please tell the others they are invited?" Angel chittered and tapped Shishi on the head to indicate for him to move. The two trotted out together.

Captain Bai asked, "Does she understand?"

"Oh, more than you realise."

He frowned as he said, "How is she supposed to tell the others when she can't speak?"

"She finds ways to get her point across." Alice didn't add anything more, as people were coming up onto the bridge.

Hara tied her hair up. "Liam says he'll stay behind. He's working on a project that he doesn't want to interrupt, but the rest of us are up for an outing."

Hara smiled at Captain Bai, who if he hadn't been so composed would have shown his shock.

Alice chuckled and went over to Shilong. "We're going to go see a game of Cuju. Any idea what that is?"

He looked at the hand she placed on his arm as he answered. "It's a game where several men chase around a ball. I have not understood the point of it but there are many who are obsessed with it."

Hara perked up. "Excellent. It'll be something different. Hey, what do you say Talen, good to get out?"

Hara directed the last to Talen who stood broodily against the wall. He grunted but otherwise didn't answer.

Gideon said, "Anyone want to bet we get into trouble?"

Hara frowned at him. "That's a horrible bet."

The two continued their conversation as they left. Captain Bai, stunned by the quickness of their departure, had to skip to catch up with them.

Shilong placed his hand on Alice's hand.

"I don't wish to offend you, but when we're out please refrain from touching me." Alice pulled her hand away as if she had been burned. She saw the hurt in Shilong's eyes but it did not show on his face.

He explained, "I do want to be with you, but you have said before you don't want others to know of our connection."

Alice blushed. She had been so quick to jump to conclusions. She just nodded her head and followed the others off the ship.

The Cuju field was larger than she had expected and it was certainly noisier. There were people cheering for the teams that went back and forth across the field. She had no idea what the rules were but she doubted it would make any more sense even if she knew them.

Talen sat next to her and Shilong. Hara, on the other side of Shilong, leaned around him and said to Talen, "Did you ever see something like this when you travelled on your own?"

Alice watched Talen silently. He was determined not to speak with Hara, which was unusual as she was normally the only person Talen talked to.

Captain Bai, sitting on her other side, tried to mitigate the awkward silence after Hara had spoken. "We've the national winners playing today against last year's winners."

Alice tried to help him push the conversation towards a safer topic. "They certainly seem determined to win."

The opposing team scored and the people in front of them jumped to their feet, surprising their group who hadn't been paying any attention at all to the game. It wasn't the game that had lured them out of the Blazing Blunderbuss, but rather the fact they were off the ship altogether.

Talen's moods had been getting worse and the fact that Murphy wasn't teasing him said more than anything. Alice glanced over and saw Susan and Murphy had their heads together and were giggling like lovesick teenagers. Alice looked at Shilong but he kept himself still. It must not be easy to be between Talen and Hara when they were obviously at odds.

Alice pointed to some monks who were in the front row. They sat calmly, unlike the other spectators. "Are they here for some reason? Because they don't look like they're having any fun."

Captain Bai shifted in his seat so he could see where she pointed. "Those are the priests who serve the dragon temple. They're here to make sure there are no riots or protestors."

Captain Bai looked to Shilong. "I thought you worked with them once."

"No."

Alice glanced at Shilong. He could be succinct, but this sounded like he was offended.

Captain Bai didn't appear to be deterred, as he continued. "I'd heard you once worked with their leader. That when there was someone who needed to be dealt with, you were called."

Shilong said, "That was never my role."

Gideon said from the other side of Hara, "There was that time when you…" Shilong shot him a look that shut him up.

Alice raised her eyebrows as she didn't know anyone that could silence Gideon when he wanted to be heard.

Shilong let out a long breath. "It's true that I have trained with those who trained the dragon priests, but I have never worked for them or done their bidding."

Alice knew he didn't like the Empress and that kind of hatred came from personal experience, so she took a risk. "What did you do for the Empress when you worked for her?"

He had mentioned he had worked for her in his youth, but he had been reluctant to speak about anything to do with that time.

Captain Bai blinked and appeared eager to hear the answer. Shilong answered after a long moment, "I don't want to talk about it."

Then he looked at Alice and let out a sigh. He spoke so only she could hear and leaned over Talen who frowned even more. "I was her executioner."

Gideon added helpfully, "He was a fixer." Shilong shot another sharp look at him but Gideon just flashed him a grin. "Our ladies aren't so squeamish, you know. We've taken on crazy fanatics before."

Alice frowned at Gideon's words. She didn't understand why he teased Shilong. Captain Bai said in a contemplative tone, "I had not realized that you no longer worked for the Empress."

Shilong settled. "Not for a long time."

It was clear he wished the conversation to be over. Hara patted Shilong's leg. "Not to worry. Everyone has a history."

Talen surprised everyone by shooting up to his feet. He snapped, "I get it already, you don't have to rub it in."

He stomped out of there. Everyone watched as he left. Hara frowned but it was clear that Talen's words had been directed to her. Alice would talk to her later about

64

Talen and his moods. Hara said, as if nothing had happened, "Captain Bai, maybe you can help us. The other day Gideon and I saw this character wandering around the city."

Gideon added, "He wasn't wandering, he was leaping in the air over whole buildings."

Hara waved off his words and continued, "He was dressed up as a monkey. Do you know who he is?"

Captain Bai frowned at the sudden change in subject, and when he looked to where Talen had left he seemed completely confused. He answered absently, "He's the Sun Wukong. The Monkey King. The Empress has been trying to catch him for years."

Gideon asked, interested, "Years? Shilong told us he has only been around for a short while."

Captain Bai shook his head and turned his attention away from Talen's exit to them. "He started in the border towns, but last year he moved his shenanigans here to the capital city."

Hara said, "He certainly seems like a character, dressed up as he is, but I don't understand why the Empress worries so much. It's only one man."

"One man who has the support of all the humans in the city. One day he could topple the Empire on his own, and the Empress is concerned about that."

Shilong said, "Not the Empress, but rather her right-hand man. The Empress has not paid attention to the running of the Empire for centuries. She wallows in the sun and reads books all day. I don't think she has even seen a court official in over a decade."

Captain Bai nodded his head in respect. "You would know better than I."

Alice studied the captain. He appeared like a competent man and it did not surprise her he had risen to the rank of captain, but she knew things were not right when it was a human soldier who was ordered to entertain them. Gideon was a dragon and related to royalty, and yet no dragon had come to see them.

———————————

Hara looked at the chickens' feet hanging from the window of a store and said to Gideon, "Do you think we'll find the rebels at all?"

Gideon said, "Unlikely. I have the feeling they're hiding from us."

Hara wondered if Shilong had anything to do with that. She was waiting for Harlen, so she didn't care that they were practically running around the city on a wild goose chase. Besides, the city was beautiful. There were stone temples and sweeping buildings that appealed to her engineering side.

It also gave Hara time to talk to Gideon when he was distracted by his search. "Do dragon babies get born like humans?"

"Oh no. Dragons lay eggs after—" He stopped and turned to look at her. He said, "Ah, I think you were asking about yourself."

Hara raised an eyebrow. "I take it then that no eggs for me?"

"No, not eggs. The pregnancy is shorter in length. The birthing is difficult but I'll be able to alleviate most of the issues."

"Gideon, I'm a little freaked at the moment but I think I need to deal with this now and think about it for a while. Just what can I expect?"

"At this stage our baby is only the size of a generous bean." He raised his hand to demonstrate, between his finger and thumb, just how big he meant. "It will grow very quickly and you'll give birth in just over six months.

The days of this planet are slightly different to our own so the timing is not exact unless you want me to work it out. Which I can." He said the last in a rushed breath when she just stared at him.

Hara was about to come to his rescue when she noticed the strange Sun Wukong creature sitting on a fountain at the end of the alley. The creature uncurled and Hara realised it was a man in a mechanical suit. He wore a mask that made him look like a monkey. His shoulders were wide and she assumed it wasn't his stature but rather a contraption. A prehensile tail made up of ringed brass moved sinuously behind him.

Hara and Gideon approached slowly. They had no idea if he was friend or foe. Considering Hara didn't know what mayhem she herself might bring to Han, she wasn't even sure if she was friend or foe.

When Sun Wukong spoke, it echoed through a machine. "You should leave."

Hara said, "The Empress is making that impossible. She wants us to find a poisoner and she has conveniently surrounded us with her military so we can't even sneak out."

"Poisoner! She is a liar." The mechanical voice had a hint of the growl of a human voice.

Gideon asked, "Do you know where we can find this person the Empress wants us to find?" Even Hara noticed the careful way he asked the question.

The tail flicked angrily and Wukong finally answered, "The Empress wants you to rout out the rebel dragons. The only deaths recently have been by her hand. If she says there is a poisoner, then she is the only suspect."

Before they could ask anything else Wukong twirled the staff in his hands, slammed it into the ground and leaped from a standstill. He leaped high and landed on the roof of the building next to them. He leaped again and was quickly out of sight.

Hara whistled, impressed. He must have had some contraption on his legs to give him that kind of lift, let alone a way to control it. She could fling things up in the air but she wouldn't be able to aim or direct where they would go. She certainly wouldn't trust any contraption enough to fling her own body up into the air like that.

She asked, "So are we going to rout out the rebels?"

"No."

Hara wasn't surprised by that. "You think there was a poisoner?"

"No."

Hara turned to look at Gideon. "So, some sightseeing?"

Gideon bowed dramatically with a flourish of his hand and offered his arm. Hara took it and Gideon said, "You truly have forgiven me, and I didn't even have to wait until you popped out the baby."

"Don't say popped. It makes me nervous." But she didn't disagree with him.

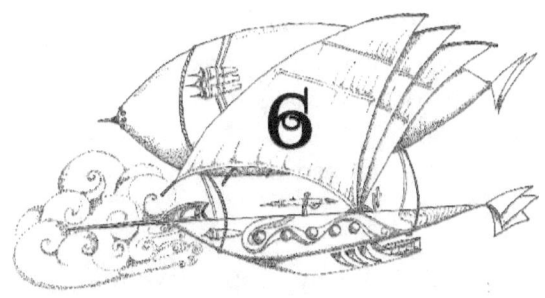

They didn't have an infirmary on the Blazing
Blunderbuss so to get the stitches taken out of
her chin she had chosen her own room.

Hermia placed her physician's bag on the table.
"Sorry, I should've taken these out days ago."

They had been in Han for over a week, but they still
hadn't gotten any closer to finishing their mission and
being able to leave. Gideon and Hara went out most days
trying to find the rebel who had attempted to poison the
Empress, but they suspected they were being used to
hunt the rebels down so didn't look particularly hard.

Hermia took out the tiniest pair of scissors Alice had
ever seen. Putting delicate fingers to Alice's chin Hermia
tilted it up. "This shouldn't take very long." She snipped
one out and stopped. "Interesting."

She moved Alice's face sideways and made
noteworthy sounds as she moved her head again, this
time tilting it forward. She moved Alice's collar aside at
the back of her neck.

Hermia sat back down, releasing Alice.
"Congratulations. I didn't realise you were thinking of
bonding with a dragon."

"What?" Alice asked, incredulous.

"You have a brand. It's very subtle."

Alice opened her mouth to ask questions but was stuck on what it all meant. The first one that came to her mind and out of her mouth was, "I'm bonded. You mean, like married?"

"Yes." Hermia looked confused, but not nearly as confused as Alice felt.

"I didn't…I mean—"

Hermia smiled. "Many people have this issue when they bond with dragons. You probably think you didn't give permission or something like that."

"Yes. He didn't even ask." Alice's voice was soft as she spoke.

"You probably did consent, but weren't aware of it. Did you talk at all about making your situation permanent, or wanting family, or feeling like you need someone to belong with?"

Alice hesitated. "Yes. I said…Ah, I said I wanted something more permanent. Are you saying I proposed to him and he accepted and now we're married? Surely it isn't that easy. There wasn't a priest or anything. It was just us."

"Usually it is. You see, dragons mate differently to humans. In human marriages you often take hands to symbolise a union. You share rings and have a ceremony. The way dragons mate is, a female dragon flies up into the air, bugling, and the men chase her. She only slows down when there is one dragon left. She matches his wing stroke and the two entwine. Then they brand each other to demonstrate they're joined to each other. So here, the dragons will chase a girl, and when they're the only one in the running they will ask for the girl's hands and brand her."

Alice thought back to her and Shilong's first night together and placed her face in her hands. Her cheeks were hot against her skin. Hermia asked nervously, "Are you regretting this? Because it's pretty awesome to be bonded to a dragon."

Alice looked up and Hermia motioned to her cheek. "You could've taken out the stitches right away after the bonding. They weren't needed at all. Let me take those out, shall I?"

Hermia snipped and took out the stitches with tweezers. Alice went over everything she knew about Shilong. Surely she hadn't missed he was a dragon.

"He has green eyes," she said. But even as she said it she knew he was a dragon, and the conversation before the Cuju game made so much sense. Captain Bai had known he was a dragon. If he had realised Shilong had mated to a human he would have reported him to the Empress.

Hermia chuckled at Alice's preoccupation. "The colour depends on what colour their scales are. We have gold and copper dragons in our part of the world. The one colour you won't see anymore is red. They were the Rosh dragons and they were utterly wiped out, down to the last dragon. I don't think the dragons would've treated with humans as well as they did if we hadn't shown we could annihilate them. For Han it's green and white colours."

Hermia had known he was a dragon, and so had Gideon. That was why Gideon had given him that look when he had first boarded the Blazing Blunderbuss.

Alice surged to her feet. "That bastard. He knew Shilong was a dragon and he didn't warn me."

Alice didn't blame Hermia; she hadn't seen Shilong until they were well on their way to Han. Gideon, on the other hand, had recognised Shilong as a dragon from the get-go. Alice didn't care about being discreet and yelled, "GIDEON!"

She charged out of the mess and yelled again, "Gideon! Where the hell are you?"

A muttered voice from the privy said, "He isn't here."

Alice found Hara leaning over a bowl and looking pale. "He went out a while ago to follow up a lead. Why do you need him? And so urgently?"

"He knew Shilong was a dragon and didn't warn anyone."

"You mean you in particular, or the whole crew?"

Alice gaped, feeling betrayed. "You knew he was a dragon!" Alice accused Hara.

"I found out just before I went to see the Empress, so don't point those sharp looks at me. You should take it up with your man...wait, dragon...whatever, you know what I mean." Hara had a point.

Alice muttered, "Shilong."

She stormed off and barged into his room. They were long past knocking. But then Alice stopped, as she wasn't sure what she was going to say.

Shilong was reading a book. He sat up at her abrupt entrance.

Alice finally found her voice. "We're married?"

He turned so he sat on the edge of the bed. He answered cautiously, "Yes."

"You're a dragon."

"Yes." He remained cautious.

"Why didn't you tell me?" Her voice showed her feeling of betrayal in its tone.

"I have my reasons."

Alice narrowed her eyes. "I want an answer, Shilong, not evasions. As your wife, surely I deserve honesty." Anger replaced all other emotion in her.

72

He stepped closer but didn't dare touch her. A wise man, as she was mad as hell. "I couldn't tell you as you might be suspicious about why a dragon needed a ride. A dragon who had once worked as an executioner for the Empress."

Yes, now she thought about it, it was suspicious that Shilong was here on the airship.

"You're an assassin for the Empress, still?" Alice asked, worried she had fallen for someone who had the morals of a snake.

"I'd never serve that serpent again," his voice was fierce.

"So you're a rebel. The same as the rebels Gideon is out looking for now?" Alice waved a hand to indicate outside the Blazing Blunderbuss.

"Yes. He won't find them."

Alice didn't doubt that for a moment. "Were you supposed to sabotage us or something if we proved to be dangerous to your people?" She was still unsure of his morals. She could live with the secrets but she worried she didn't know him at all.

"I knew right from the beginning when I met Hara and Gideon that they were honourable and I would not have to harm them. I wouldn't have...I wouldn't have bonded with you if I had thought I would have to harm your friends."

"You're darn right."

He said in a soft voice, "Are you angry with me?"

"Yes." Alice knew anger was only part of what she felt.

"Will you be able to forgive me?" He lifted his hands up in a pleading gesture.

"I don't know." She stormed out.

Hara stood by the privy and looked a lot better. It was a good thing morning sickness didn't linger too long for her. Hara said, "You should get him to apologise now."

"Why?" Alice wanted to yell or throw something but managed to contain her anger.

"Trust me. You're mad at him at the moment and apologies are best when you're mad."

"He betrayed me. Tricked me. Lied to me. I think I'll be mad with him for a while." She could barely even think of Shilong without anger filling her.

"You'd think that'd be the truth." Hara shrugged.

Alice realised that Hara was talking about herself. She was sure that she, Alice, would be different. Even now she couldn't hold the anger.

Alice asked, "Are they always like this?"

Hara chuckled. "Oh yeah."

Alice turned around and returned to Shilong's room. The door was still open from when she had stormed out. She pointed a finger at him. "No more lies, and you tell Gideon what he needs to know so we can get the hell out of here where there are crazy she-dragons making us chase assassins around the city."

"We did not poison the Empress. None of us would be able to bring rampion across the void." He was still standing in the same place she had left him. She knew she hadn't been gone long but she frowned as she realised this small fact.

He said softly, "I'm not a cad like your old beau."

No, he was very different. Hara was right. She had to ride this emotion until it fizzed out, which it was already threatening to do.

She huffed out a breath. "I want new boots."

Shilong bowed his head. Feeling perverse, she added, "And a new dress." Not that she wanted or needed a new dress, but she wanted to punish him and maybe set a precedent. Dragons saw objects as having their own inherent value. He would understand what she was asking for when she wanted repayment.

"Something that brings out the green of your eyes." His voice showed his relief.

Alice let go of the last of the mad. "Yes. With pockets. It has to have pockets." She spun on her heels.

Shilong said quietly, "I am sorry. I was dishonourable." Hara was right. An apology was better when you were still mad.

As she arrived on the bridge in the early evening, Hara asked, "Has Gideon returned?"

Alice answered, "No," and she was worried.

Gideon and Hara had never been out after dark. Hara went to the window of the bridge. Alice was on watch but everyone else was playing games in the mess. Angel and Shishi came up to Hara. Hara reached down and ran a hand over Shishi's head.

Alice asked, "Do you want me and Shilong to go look for him?" Shilong would be useful wandering the streets in Yeijing.

Hara shook her head. "We'll wait."

But Hara could hear the nerves in her own voice. It would be a long wait. Susan arrived on the bridge and plonked a tray of freshly baked cookies on the navigation table. "I think we need some of this."

Susan looked at Shilong. "Go along. We need some time with just us girls."

Shilong hesitated and checked with Alice before he ducked off the bridge. Susan said, "Sometimes we need to bolster ourselves with some sugar."

Alice asked, "Bolster ourselves for what? For realising that Gideon is missing, or that Shilong is a spy for the rebels?"

Hara said, "I think he was sent here to make sure Gideon wasn't going to work against the rebels. I think they came to some understanding and Shilong decided to change his mission."

Alice asked, "What mission?"

Hara shrugged. "From what Gideon said, probably assassination."

Susan chuckled and passed Alice a cookie. "Congratulations, you're married to an assassin."

Alice took the cookie and crammed the whole thing into her mouth. Susan held the tray away. "Easy there, girl. You want to be happy, not sick."

"It's just a cookie. How much sugar can it have?"

Susan raised an eyebrow. "A couple of cups. It's easy to get hold of sugar this close to the equator." Alice motioned for Susan to pass over another cookie.

Hara said, "Don't blame Shilong. He's probably just trying to protect you."

"That is just drivel we women tell ourselves when men are being arrogant."

Hara laughed richly. She even mopped tears from her eyes and eventually said, "Alice, he's a dragon. He isn't human, and I'm afraid the only thing all dragons have in common is that they are all supremely arrogant."

"Even Gideon?" Alice asked, stunned that Hara had anything bad to say about her mate.

"Oh, definitely him." Hara didn't hesitate.

"Shilong isn't like Gideon. He's calm." Alice took a bite and this time savoured the cookie.

"Doesn't mean he isn't arrogant."

"He could've told me." Even Alice could hear the whine in her voice.

Hara shrugged and took the cookie Susan offered but didn't eat it. She looked a bit pale. Was her morning sickness back?

"You know that it's illegal for Shilong to get married, don't you? The Empress refuses to mate with her dragons but she doesn't want them with anyone else. Shilong is showing a lot of trust in you by bonding with you. You could turn him in and you could walk away free. It mustn't be easy to live in this place." She waved to indicate Han. She stopped talking abruptly and pursed her lips. "Got to go."

She dashed off the bridge.

Susan said, "That morning sickness really is kicking her butt at the moment. I heard the pregnancy isn't as long. Maybe the morning sickness won't last as long." Susan turned to Alice. "At least you can see what it's like for when you start popping out the munchkins yourself."

Alice spluttered out bits of cookie and decided to put the cookie down as she was suddenly not very steady. Susan looked on in concern.

Alice said, "It's nothing, but I think I might head to bed as well. Is it your shift?"

"No, Murphy's on tonight. I told him to wait a bit, that I thought you guys needed some girl talk."

Alice shook her head. Susan wasn't wrong, but there was so much else going on. It was unfortunate, as Alice thought Hara could do with some quiet time to deal with her pregnancy. Alice needed the time herself. Gideon and even Shilong had admitted that dragons bonded with humans were prolific.

Alice said her farewells to Susan and left the bridge. She almost went to her own room but she stopped outside Shilong's and knocked softly.

He opened the door. She said before he could ask anything, "We need to talk. You need to tell me everything about yourself. I need to know who I'm married to and I have to tell you I'm not ready for babies. Not yet."

Shilong said, "Dragons can choose when to have children."

Alice hoped Hara never found that out, or Gideon might find himself being dragged behind the Blazing Blunderbuss in chains for a week.

Everyone was up early and in the mess. Susan had made a generous pot of coffee. It tasted terrible and bitter but it was what they needed. There were no cookies left; Alice suspected the boys had polished those off last night while she had spoken with Shilong till the early morning.

Alice asked, "Should we wake Hara?" The others all looked around at each other. It was clear everyone was on edge, wanting to do something.

Liam said, "Let her sleep. Though I doubt she's sleeping well."

Probably, which made Alice wonder where their captain was. Without a word she got to her feet and went to Hara's room. She cracked the door just a little to look inside. The bed was made. In fact, it looked like no one had slept there at all. Alice opened the door more.

There was a note on the table. Alice knew it wasn't just a piece of scrap. Hara was very particular about how to clean up things. She never left anything out. Alice went into the empty room and looked down at the note.

"Gone looking for Gideon. Back soon."

That had probably been written the previous night. "Soon" had since passed. Cursing softly, Alice grabbed the note and stormed back to the mess.

Alice waved the note as she entered the room. "She's gone."

Murphy sighed. "Probably shanghaied, like Gideon."

Alice nodded and let her thoughts calm so she could get a handle on what was happening. "They must have been waiting for Gideon to be on his own. The same with Hara."

The two had been out searching for over a week. If the kidnappers were going to abduct them it could have been any time in that week. Obviously, they wanted Gideon or Hara to be alone.

"We'll stay in pairs. Shilong, do you think it was the rebels?"

"No, but we can ask."

Alice nodded. "Shilong and I will go to the rebels. Murphy and Talen, you'll go to the place Gideon went missing."

Even if Gideon didn't keep notes about where he was going, Hara did, and it would be in the log book on the bridge.

Alice indicated Susan. "You'll stay here with Liam. If it was the Empress who took Gideon, then it might not be a good idea for us to stay nestled among the military. Make some excuse, say you're testing new engines or something and move the Blazing Blunderbuss. Just fly it around the city. We'll all take flares and if we get in trouble we'll let those off. You can come get us."

Susan nodded her head. She certainly had more gumption than Henry, their previous cook. He might have run with pirates for awhile but he was a gentle soul.

Not Susan. She had been living among whalers in the southern oceans. She had not been a whore, but rather worked on one of the ships.

Talen said, "Who died and made you captain?" There was a gasp from someone at the table, but Alice wasn't sure who.

Raising an eyebrow, Alice asked Talen, "You're choosing now to cause trouble? The captain and Gideon are missing. They're by far the biggest hitters on this ship." Alice almost expected Murphy to complain about having all the guns, but he must have realised how important this conversation was as he remained silent.

Talen had been fighting his place here on the Blazing Blunderbuss while the others had settled in comfortably. Alice knew it had to do with his previous life, where he hadn't needed to answer to anyone. Hara had explained to Alice that Talen was looking for a new life, otherwise he would have left a long time ago. For Hara's sake Alice would give Talen the benefit of the doubt.

She leaned forward before Talen could answer her rather rhetorical question. "We're all part of a collection. I don't particularly care who's in charge at the moment, Talen, but I do know one thing. Hara trusts me. You, I'm not too sure about. We're going after them. Do you disagree with that plan?"

"No." She could see he was conflicted as the word was dragged out.

"Do you think we should search separately?"

"No." This time his answer was more sure.

"Do you think we should split off into different groups?"

He took longer to answer this one as he thought about the pairs Alice had divided them into.

"No."

"Then what are you complaining about? That a woman is in charge? As Hara is a woman, you know, so nothing different there. That I don't have the right? Because I'm the first mate. That means I'm in charge until Hara gets back. It's always been that way."

Talen pursed his lips. He was about to sulk but Alice wanted to resolve this and give him something to think about.

She straightened and added, "Think, Talen, about why you object, because I believe it has more to do with you rather than me or even this situation."

Alice was tempted to add more but at that moment Liam came into the mess. He looked around and then, with a frown creasing his brow, asked, "Has anyone seen Angel or the foo-lion?"

Alice swore. "Hara's gone missing. She left last night to look for Gideon. They must be with her."

That was a good thing. Angel was resourceful and it wouldn't be the first time she had rescued Hara when she was in a pinch.

Liam asked Alice, "What's the plan, first mate?" It was a reminder to Talen that she did have the right to take over, and a good one as it came from someone who hadn't been part of the conversation before.

Alice said, "Glad you asked."

<hr/>

Shilong leaned against the doorway while Alice sorted out things on the bridge for her departure. There were papers they would need to file with the dock before the Blazing Blunderbuss could move an inch, and although Liam and Susan were willing to take the ship for a ride, they had no idea how to fill in the forms.

Alice looked up when she caught Shilong watching her. She stopped and returned his look.

He said into the silence, "It's illegal for a dragon to have a human mate."

"I know. Hara told me." That made his insistence that they didn't show affection to each other in public much more understandable, even though it was what she had requested as well.

"Do you know what they'll do to you if we're caught?" He wasn't to be distracted from the point he wanted to make.

"No. They won't kill me, will they?" From anything but death there was always a way out.

"No, but you might wish it. They'll torture you, and with the gift of my kind you'll heal fast, so they can torture you for days on end without ceasing."

Alice leaned on the table she had been working on and studied Shilong. He was genuinely concerned.

"I'm a foreigner, and I know while I'm here I fall under your laws, but that should make a difference."

"It won't. You'll eventually be forced to divorce me and they'll let you go and I'll stay underground where they'll bury me." His face betrayed his pain for just a moment.

Alice said, "It might not seem it now, but I do have friends who'll come for me if that happens. Don't worry about something that hasn't happened yet."

He stepped up closer to her, moving away from the door. "I don't want to lose you."

Shilong didn't often show his emotions. Usually, it was when they were in bed, but Alice could hear in his voice he wanted her to understand how serious this was. Alice closed the space between them and picked up his hands. He glanced down and frowned, a little confused.

The Han were not a very tactile people, and taking hands was not something done often.

Alice said, "I'm not like the women here, Shilong."

"I know. It's why I chose you."

She shook her head. "You're missing the point. I'm not a Han woman who is afraid to leave the country to be with someone I love."

"You love me?" his voice broke as he asked.

"Yes. I wouldn't have stayed that first night if I didn't feel something."

"I don't want to see you hurt." His green eyes sparked with his determination.

"Well, once we get the captain and Gideon back, we can leave Han and not worry about having to deal with the Empress." She didn't want to be hurt either, but they couldn't leave Hara and Gideon to whomever had them.

Shilong looked thoughtful and admitted, "Hara has mentioned that I might stay on the Blazing Blunderbuss."

Alice chuckled. "Yeah, we can always do with more crew. We're short about five crew for a ship this size. You can help Liam in the engine room."

He frowned and she chuckled. "Don't worry, it isn't shovelling coal. The captain has a better way to produce steam. I think you might be interested. Talk to Liam later. In the meantime, let's go talk to your rebels."

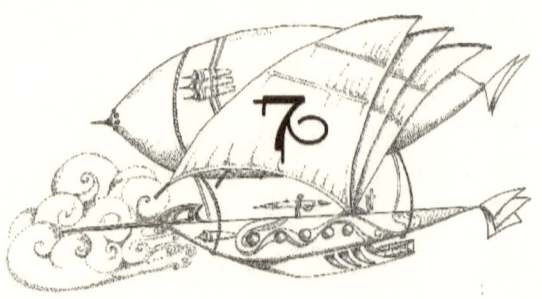

Alice was usually very good at navigation but she was completely lost. They had travelled on a tram and then on foot through winding streets. They had turned left and right so many times that the only way Alice knew which way the Blazing Blunderbuss was, was because she could still see the sun sinking down over the buildings.

It had taken longer to find the rebels than expected. It wasn't a matter of just heading into the city and going to a meeting place. Shilong had to first send a message, and they had had to wait for a reply before they told him where they could meet someone willing to talk to them. Apparently Shilong had been out of the country long enough that they didn't wholly trust him. Shilong hadn't seemed slighted that his own people didn't trust him.

Shilong stopped. "I think this is the place."

Alice asked, "You think? Weren't the directions very clear?"

Shilong studied the building. She could understand his lack of confidence. The building was like all the others in this neighborhood. The only thing that differentiated it from the other buildings on the block was a sign painted on the mantel above the door. It was in Han letters, which Alice couldn't read, but next to it was a small piece of quartz embedded in the wood. Alice knew the quartz was important to dragons, but more as a deterrent. Hara wouldn't let them transport quartz, ebony or ivory, though Alice wasn't entirely sure why. Only that it had something to do with dragons.

Alice said, "Are you worried about something? That the rebels might do something?"

"We're so angry." Considering she had found out it was illegal for dragons in Han to be married, she could imagine why. She wasn't sure why that would make him nervous to see his own kind. "We have been so angry for so long that the kindness in us is no longer there. I would not wish for you to be hurt."

"You think they would injure me or kill me?"

"No, they are more likely to use words." Alice looked at Shilong with confusion. Was he really concerned about her feelings?

Alice said, "Shilong, do you think I'm a strong person?"

"Yes. Of course." She liked that he didn't hesitate.

"Then trust me when I say I can handle anything your rebel dragons are about to throw at me." She hoped she wasn't making a liar out of herself, but she knew that no matter what they faced she could handle it. If she could handle having to leave her home because her ex had turned everyone against her, she could handle meeting rebel dragons.

Shilong hesitated, but eventually he went up to the door and knocked in the way he had been instructed. The door opened automatically. There wasn't anyone on the other side but the slight click of gears told Alice the door was opened using automation. It was dark inside but she wasn't surprised by that. Dragons liked to be dramatic.

She headed in even before Shilong. She wasn't sure why he was so hesitant, but they had to get some answers if they were going to find Gideon and Hara. She didn't want to think of what could have happened to them in the day that Gideon had been missing.

The door closed behind them with a soft click and plunged them into darkness. A voice said out of the darkness, "Speak."

Shilong said, "You don't have to put on the act, Xu, I know it's you."

Light flickered and there was a small lantern on a table next to the man. He was dressed in a military uniform, so he was being cautious by hiding himself in the dark.

He looked up from the lantern. "Shi, you look well." It was a kind greeting, but Alice didn't feel any love between the two.

Alice decided she would see if Xu was more pleasant to her. "I'm Alice. We're looking for our captain and her mate Gideon."

"It wasn't us."

Alice shrugged. "We thought as much. You're in a position to know a little more than we do about what's happening in Yeijing."

Xu studied her then looked at Shilong. He said something in Han and Shilong replied in Imperial, "She is my mate."

Xu shook his head. "You're a fool, Shi. The Empress will throw you into a hole and your mate will die of old age before you'll see daylight again."

Shilong shook his head. "She's honourable, she will not betray me. Will you?"

The Empress made women divorce their mates and left them to rot in some prison while the women went on with their lives. Alice could understand how the dragons could perceive it differently. Their lives were so long that they would see the whole process as an early demise for their mates.

Alice decided to get the conversation back on track. "Do you know anything about the kidnappings?"

Xu shrugged. "There are many who disappear in Yeijing. Who am I to say who took them?"

Shilong hissed. "You are fools."

"You were supposed to eliminate the dragon."

Alice glanced at Shilong, but she wouldn't reveal her surprise. Instead she watched as Shilong said, "Gideon isn't the dragon we should eliminate."

Xu scoffed. "You would advocate killing one of the few female dragons on this planet? You would doom us to death?"

"No, the hybrids are our future." Shilong's calm façade dropped for a moment as he spoke fiercely.

Xu flicked a hand to indicate Alice. "This is your choice? A pale round-eye?"

"Yes," Shilong said without any hesitation.

Xu shrugged. "Then you really are a fool."

Alice said, "If we're finished with the insulting-the-foreigner part of the conversation, are you going to tell us anything or not?"

There was a long silence and it was clear Xu wasn't going to give any answer. Eventually Shilong said, "You'll regret being so prudent."

Shilong caught Alice's arm and stepped back towards the closed door. Xu extinguished the light as the door softly whirred open. Alice blinked at the bright light outside.

"I apologise for not upholding your honour. He insulted you and I should have challenged him for that."

"No need. If I wanted someone to go all macho on me, I'd have picked Murphy instead of you."

She realised he was unsure of her by the sharp look he gave her.

He said in a soft voice, "Did you truly choose me? You were so angry I had thought—"

Alice shook her head. "You hid things from me, but that doesn't change the fact that I came to your room and asked for something more permanent."

It was not something she would regret any time soon. Alice wouldn't have said that yesterday, but she had spoken with Hara and Hermia for a while until she had sorted out the twisted feelings inside her. Shilong was offering her a future she wanted, and everything she had seen of him indicated that he was a good man. She wasn't sure if it was the forever kind of relationship, but she was willing to see how far it would go.

Besides, she trusted Hara and Hermia's instincts on men. Alice's first choice had turned out to be a bad egg and she had known him since they were children.

Shilong was the one to spot the man on the roof of a building in the distance. "There is Sun Wukong."

"If the rebels don't know where the captain is, maybe the monkey does." Alice pulled up her skirts and started running. Her quick action startled Shilong, but he managed to catch up with her and motioned down an alley so they would be able to catch up with the man. He wore a contraption that allowed him to leap from rooftop to rooftop with apparent ease.

Alice was soon puffing with effort. She had thought she was keeping fit on the airship but she was obviously delusional. She stopped to take a breath. Shilong stopped when he realised she was falling behind. He frowned but she waved off his concern.

Alice was about to ask him his opinion on leaving Sun Wukong alone when shadows dropped down from the roof of nearby buildings. Shilong growled, but before he could do anything a net was thrown over him. Another was thrown over her, and the weight of the heavy rope trapped them on the ground. Alice wriggled under the net to see who had ambushed them. They were dressed a lot like Xu except their uniforms were predominantly green.

Shilong must have recognised them because he yelled, "Jade guard! Let us go, we have done no harm to you or yours."

One of the men squatted in front of Shilong. "You're a traitor. That's all we need to know. The Empress will be pleased to have you and your tramp."

Shilong swore and tried to move but the net hampered him.

<hr />

They dumped Alice unceremoniously on a cold stone floor. They had tied her up like a pig for market but she managed to take the hit of the ground on her shoulder instead of her face. Shilong was thrown on the ground next to her but he was still trussed up in the net.

He shifted so he could see her and asked quietly, "Are you alright?"

"I'm just dandy," she answered sarcastically. "No, of course I'm not. I've been tied up like an animal ready for slaughter by a bunch of sex-starved dragons."

"Very touching," one of the dragons that had captured them said in a drawl. He crouched over them. "The stakes aren't going to be very good on the betting books for this one. I wonder if she'll last the day."

Shilong growled. "Enlai, you leave her alone. I swear if you hurt her, I'll break your neck."

"If you're trying to convince us she isn't bonded to you, you aren't doing a very good job." Enlai straightened and motioned to one of the others. Shilong struggled in the net to free himself.

Enlai said to his man, "Strip her so we can see if she has a brand."

Shilong thrashed around, and Alice had to agree that being helpless while several men crowded around her with the express purpose of getting her naked was not something she wanted. She wriggled but they had tied her up well.

One dragon pulled a knife and caught the cloth of her dress at the front and lifted her up easily. Shilong made a sound like a wounded animal. "No, check me. Check me. I swear, Enlai, I'll make you pay if you put one finger on her."

The man holding Alice hesitated and Enlai said, "Are you sure, Shilong? That means we'll have to necklace you. No fighting back, no changing."

Shilong went limp. It was his only sign of capitulation. Enlai motioned to the man holding Alice. He dropped her, and not gently. He disappeared out of her view and when he returned, he had a considerably large cuff. He kicked and shoved Shilong around and threaded the cuff through the net and wrapped it around Shilong's neck.

There was an ominous click.

They then took the net off Shilong and roughly stripped him of his clothes. They flipped him on his stomach to see the brand that covered his back. Alice had seen it before, but that had been before she had known they were married and what the brand had really meant. She had thought it was just an elaborate tattoo of a dragon flying through clouds. The head was at the top of

Shilong's spine and the tail wrapped around his right leg almost to his knee.

The leader of the Jade Guard, Enlai, said, "Quite elaborate. I wouldn't have considered you a sentimental type, Shilong." He turned to Alice. "The larger and the more elaborate the brand is, the more emotion there was in the dragon when the brand was made." He indicated to Shilong. "The boy is in love."

Then he said to his men, "Put him in the hole. I want to talk to his woman for a bit."

When the men dragged Shilong to his feet he was limp in their arms, and they shoved him out of the room. Enlai pulled over a stool and sat by Alice's head. He pulled out a knife, but Alice could recognise the tactic for what it was. Because of the added healing ability she received by being Shilong's mate, killing her would be a long and arduous business with a mere knife. The weapon was purely to intimidate, and unfortunately it was working. Alice wasn't a fan of pain.

She tried to shift off the shoulder she had landed on. Enlai kicked her over so she was on her back, but now her hands were trapped underneath her and pain radiated from both her shoulders. She must have shown her pain as Enlai purred, "A bit delicate. It won't take long to break you."

He leaned forward, resting his elbows on his knees, and started twirling the knife. He watched the blade rather than Alice. "We haven't had a dragon stupid enough to bond with a woman in almost a decade. She broke in a week. A little disappointing, as I prefer when they wait until I take a limb. We leave amputation for the second month. We find few last much longer than that."

He pointed the blade at her. "We'll let you think overnight, and when tomorrow comes we'll start the fun part. We're going to cut off that brand. Strip by strip."

He placed the blade against her cheek where the only visible part of her brand showed. Alice flinched back. He chuckled and stood up. He kicked away the stool and motioned to one of the guards. "Take her away."

Two men, including the guard, lifted her up and carried her further into the complex and threw her into one of the cells. This time it hurt more as they swung her back and gave her a bit more momentum, and she slid into the wall on the other side of the small cell. They slammed the gate shut and didn't even bother to untie her.

Alice concentrated on her body and relaxed as much as possible. Soon the ache in her arms reduced and she was able to doze. She hoped they weren't doing horrible things to Shilong.

A skittering and then the sound of metal against metal woke her up. She was hungry, so she assumed it was some time later. It was light, so it was probably the next day.

Xu stood by the gate. "I warned you."

"If you're just going to stand there spouting gloom and doom then you can bugger off."

He frowned, and she wondered if it was because of her tone. The Han did not expect a lot of emotion from their women, but she wasn't Han, and she was tied up in a prison so she had a perfect excuse to be sharp.

He pulled a knife. "Come closer. I can at least untie you." She shuffled so he could reach through the bars and cut her bonds.

It was painful to have blood return to places that had been cut off by the tight rope. She remained lying on the ground as it was too painful to move after she was freed. She looked up at Xu. "Is that all you can do?"

He shrugged. Alice grunted. "Not much of a rebel then."

"You're human. Your lives are fleeting."

"I'm bonded to Shilong. I'll live as long as he will," Alice countered his argument easily.

"You'll divorce him just like all the others. They gave up on their men."

"It doesn't have to be that way." She wasn't a fool. She knew if they started sawing off one of her legs she was going to cave.

Xu stood stiffly. "You don't understand."

He turned to leave and she called out to him. "You'll have to choose soon, Xu. You and the rest of you, as you won't be able to sit on the fence."

He didn't hesitate as he walked off angrily. Alice laid her head back down and sighed. Apparently convincing stubborn Han men wasn't one of her talents.

She looked up when she heard the click of metal on stone. Shishi and Angel strolled down the corridor. Moving quickly to her knees, Alice reached through the bars. "Oh, it's so good to see you, Angel."

Shishi stopped in front of her and dropped something out of his mouth. Angel chittered. It was keys. Tears pricked Alice's eyes, but she rapidly gathered herself and scooped up the keys.

She spoke to Angel and Shishi as she worked on the lock. "They've taken Shilong. We have to get him back. I don't know what they're going to do to him if they find me gone." The lock clicked and she shoved the door open.

She turned to the clockwork creatures. She hoped Hara was alright and back at the Blazing Blunderbuss and that was why Angel had been able to come after her, but she didn't want to ask and receive an answer in the negative. So instead, she clamped down on her curiosity. "Right. Let's rescue Shilong. Shishi, lead the way."

———◆———

Harlen landed on the lake shore and placed Lala in front of him before he changed to his human form. Lala looked around the palace gardens. "It's beautiful."

"It was built on the backs of slaves." His voice was rough as he was still mostly dragon.

She rolled her eyes. "No need to sound so superior, Harlen. All countries were built on the back of slaves, even if they weren't called slaves but peasants instead." She was astounded he was so vehement about slavery.

Lala took the time to look at the architecture. The buildings in Han had been made for flying over more than buildings in the Wyvern Empire, but they hadn't been flying slowly enough for her to take in the architecture. The small island was filled with stunning buildings of bright colours and sweeping roof lines.

Harlen finished dressing and strutted towards the buildings. Lala skipped to keep up with his wide stride. "Do you think it'll be alright to pop in like this? We haven't got an invitation."

"You worry about things that are not worth worrying about."

"Does that mean we'll be welcomed?" There was amusement in her voice. She really did enjoy arguing with him.

"That's highly unlikely. I told you I don't like Han."

"What does that have to do with us being welcomed? Oh no, don't tell me you've been here before and caused trouble."

"I wouldn't call it trouble."

Lala snorted and slowed down as she caught up with him. Harlen didn't wait for any invitation of any sort and walked through the palace to a sizable courtyard. There was a green dragon curled up in the space. The dragon was massive; larger than any dragon she had ever seen.

Harlen said, "Where is my brother?"

The dragon seemed startled, as it went very still for a moment before uncurling its head to turn to look at Harlen. "Dragons don't have siblings. I assume you are speaking about the lost prince. I haven't done anything to your brother, you rude thing."

Lala gaped. She had never heard of a dragon that could speak in its dragon form. It also meant this could only be the Jade Empress. The dragon uncurled some more and flicked a claw towards Harlen. "Now go away, you annoying thing."

Harlen said, "You summoned my brother here, so that makes you responsible for anything that happens to him while he is in your territory."

"Is that a threat, peasant?"

"Yes. We might have been peasants back on our planet, but we're the largest collection on this planet and we could wipe out you and your kind easily."

The Jade Empress slammed her claw down and blew hot air over the two of them. Lala frowned and looked at Harlen. She had been hoping to see if he was nervous or not, then she remembered that he never showed his emotions. She looked at the dragon and wondered for a moment whether Harlen would actually get her eaten by a dragon after all. She hadn't been worried about that for months now.

"I have not brought harm to your brother, little prince." It was a big leap from peasant to prince, but

Harlen's connection to the Wyvern Empire was undeniable. There were few who had as much power as Harlen.

"Then are you aware that he was kidnapped two days ago?"

The Jade Empress settled back. "No."

"You aren't looking after your collection very well, Empress."

"They are my subjects. They're there to serve me. They're not in my collection."

Harlen said in a deceptively calm voice, "That isn't how it works, Empress, and you know it. You better look out, or someone might come in and take your whole collection."

Harlen stepped back just as the Empress lunged at him. Lala was startled, but she had been training with Harlen for a while now and moved without thought. She somersaulted out of the way.

The Empress growled. "What is this? A dragon hunter?" Then she yelled, "YOU BROUGHT A DRAGON HUNTER TO MY HOME!"

Harlen was still calm. "She is my mate."

The Empress screamed and it shook the walls.

Harlen came over to where Lala stood and caught up her arm. "We better go."

He started moving and it was at a faster pace than usual, so Lala had to jog to keep up with him.

Lala asked, "Was that necessary?"

"Yes." He dodged to the side and pulled her along.

Some soldiers poured from one of the corridors. Harlen picked up the pace and Lala was now running.

She glanced back at the soldiers. "Is this what happened the last time you were in Han?"

Harlen took a moment to think about his answer before he said, "Pretty much."

Shishi and Angel led Alice deep into the palace. The rooms below street level were damp and very suitable for dungeons as far as Alice was concerned. There weren't many guards, which amazed her. Shishi stopped at a door and looked up at her expectantly. Alice just looked back, and Angel chittered as she motioned to the door. Alice winced. Obviously they wanted her to open the door.

The door was heavy and it creaked as she shoved it open. She stepped back for the clockwork creatures to enter first, but they just stood there looking at her anxiously.

Alice went inside the room. It was dark and filled with holes in the floor which were covered in grates.

Frowning, Alice called out quietly, "Shilong?" There was a groan, and Alice moved further into the room and realised there were people in the holes.

Alice glanced back at Shishi and Angel but they were gone. She muttered something about them sneaking off but decided that it was more important to search the holes.

Kneeling by the first one, she called down, "Shilong."

The man that answered said, "I'm not Shilong, but if you're here to rescue your man would you release us all?"

Alice hesitated. She wasn't sure why these men had been imprisoned, but she was also practical. She intended to escape from the palace, and if the guards were chasing other escaped prisoners her chances of escape increased.

The grates were kept shut with pins that were impossible for the men inside to reach. She pulled the pin from the grate the voice had come from and flipped it open. "You'll have to do the rest yourself."

A head popped out of the hole. His eyes were a pale pearl colour. A dragon. His voice was soft as he spoke. "We will."

He crawled out of the hole. He was mostly skin and bone. She had no idea how long he had been down there, but considering that the last dragon to be married to a human in Han was over a decade before, it could be as long.

She went to all the grates and opened them up. The other holes had dragons as well, but most of them spoke to her in Han instead of in Imperial as the first man had.

She kept calling for Shilong. One of the men pointed down a corridor and she had to assume he was indicating where Shilong was.

There was a single room at the end of the corridor. It was dominated by a table and Shilong was tied to it, and he bled because they had literally nailed him to the table.

Alice put her hand to her mouth to hold in the sob. Shilong groaned and she moved quickly then. She rushed over to the table and tried to pull out the huge metal nails but her hands slipped on the blood.

She looked around as Shilong said gently, "Alice?"

She shushed him. "Quiet, Shilong. I'm going to get you out of here." She had to blink back tears, as this was not the time to give into sentimentality. For him to go through all this just so they wouldn't strip her naked. She would have preferred to have danced buck naked in front of the Empress than for him to suffer like this just for her sake.

She found a weird-shaped tool, a bit like a claw hammer without the hammer part. She wedged it under the head of one nail and pulled it up. Shilong cried out in pain and Alice whimpered in sympathy.

She put her hand on the wound to stop the blood but she could feel under her hand as his body started to heal. That explained why they had left the nails in, as dragons could heal surprisingly fast.

Alice went to the next nail and pulled it out. She didn't try to stem the blood flow, but rather went to the next and then the next. She dropped the nails on the floor or flung them away when Shilong cried out with pain and she needed to show her frustration.

Once all of the nails were out Alice helped Shilong to sit up. His hands tightened on her arms. "Alice? You're free." His voice was muzzy with his own confusion. He had once told her all the women taken had broken the bond to their dragon mate.

She reassured him, "We're still bonded."

His words were filled with awe. "I know. I can feel the bond. But how? How did you get free?"

"Shishi brought me some keys. I take it he's going to be joining our motley crew." She didn't ask if Shilong intended to join them. He was still naked from when the Jade Guard had checked for the mating brand.

Alice asked, "Do you have any clothes?"

She knew dragons could keep things in another place. He answered by putting his hand on the table next to him, and clothes appeared. Alice looked at the blood that covered him and searched around for a cloth. Shilong didn't move. He just breathed deeply.

She found something and wiped as much of the blood off as she could. She then helped Shilong to dress. He panted with pain afterwards. She wasn't sure if the guards had done something else to him, but they needed to escape the palace before anyone could do anything else.

Alice helped him by wrapping an arm around his waist, and the two of them headed out of the torture chamber. Shilong glanced at the holes. "You let the others go?"

"Yes. They should distract the guards." He frowned, and she wondered what she had said that bothered him.

When they got to the edge of the island, Lala said as she huffed for breath, "What are we going to do? We can't just keep running all day."

Staring at the shore of the lake on the other side of the water, Harlen asked, "Do you trust me?"

Lala answered without hesitation, "Yes."

Harlen turned to look at her sharply. She shrugged. "That isn't the issue between us, Harlen. You know that. Now, do you have a plan to get out of here?"

Harlen frowned, but he didn't say anything about their relationship though Lala knew he wanted to settle what was between them. Being chased by soldiers through a palace wasn't the time.

Harlen offered his hand. "This is going to hurt, but if you trust me, it should hurt less." She wasn't sure if that was just a line he used but she took his hand and stepped into his personal space.

Before she could ask what he intended to do, she was thrown into an eternal darkness that sapped away her breath. She tried to drag in a lungful but there was nothing there to breathe with. Lala wasn't Lala; she was just a thought. Then Lala was Lala again, and she coughed and gasped as she tried to breathe in when her body tried to breathe out and she just hiccupped spit instead.

When she finally got her breath, she turned to Harlen. "What the hell was that?"

Harlen's answer was to point over the water. She realised she was looking at the palace building they had left on the other side of the water. She could see the soldiers milling on the shore trying to find a way to cross.

Lala turned to Harlen and said sharply, "I didn't know dragons could do that." As a dragon hunter, Lala was fully aware of what dragons could do. If dragons could pop out of the world and back in with their collections, like they had just done, she would have heard of it.

Harlen shrugged. "Gideon and I figured it out years ago. We realised we ourselves are part of our own collections and we should be able to treat our human bodies like we do our collections. It doesn't work over a large distance, but as long as it's within sight I can move myself and you, as you are in my collection."

Lala was about to ask for an answer that wasn't completely confusing when a foo-lion approached them, a small clockwork dragon riding on its back. Lala doubted the Empress would allow a clockwork creature that looked like a dragon to be anywhere in the Han empire. Harlen seemed to recognise the creature and crouched down to greet it, confirming to Lala that things were not as they seemed.

Harlen said, "Angel? What are you doing here? Where's your master?"

The clockwork dragon clicked its mouth and chittered excitedly. It waved its small claws and pointed back to where it had come from. Harlen nodded and straightened up.

He turned to Lala. "We have a guide." Lala shook her head, amazed by Harlen's encounter with the creature.

Lala asked, "What is it?"

"It's a she, and she belongs to Hara's collection. She wants us to follow her." He pointed, as Angel had disappeared. "That way."

Lala smiled. "You really do like Hara. Should I be jealous?"

Harlen frowned seriously. "I would never dishonour you that way."

Lala shook her head at his inability to be teased. "I know, Harlen. We better hurry. Your clockwork friend is eager for us to follow." She said this as Angel and her foo-lion were almost out of view. Harlen nodded and the two of them jogged after the two clockwork creatures into the maze that made up the summer palace complex.

◆————————————◆

Alice tightened her hold on Shilong as they limped through the narrow corridors. They moved as quietly as possible but they could hear the released prisoners causing trouble. Alice had no idea how to navigate a way out of the palace. Even Shilong was not familiar with the twisting corridors that made up the prison section of the palace.

A foo-lion came around the corner and for a moment Alice thought it was Shishi. When it gave a silent roar and charged, she realised she was wrong.

Alice pushed Shilong aside. He was in no shape to fight anything, even a large metal dog.

The foo-lion bowled her over. The mechanical creature was badly designed as it couldn't open its mouth wide enough to bite her. It rammed her with its head but it was fairly useless as an attack dog. Alice shoved it off her and got to her feet.

When it charged again, she kicked it out of the way. Pain shot up her leg and then faded quickly, but she hopped on one foot as it did. She had forgotten the silly things were made out of metal.

Shilong leaned against the wall. He snapped something to the foo-lion and it backed up. It shook its head and backed up some more. Shilong said something else and it turned and left them.

Alice didn't ask what he had told the mechanical beast to make it to leave them alone. They had to return to the Blazing Blunderbuss and the Jade Guard had taken their flares from them. So that meant they would have to rescue themselves.

Alice heard footsteps and pulled Shilong into the shadows of a doorway. They waited for a moment until it was silent again. Shilong whispered, "Did they harm you?"

"No. I'm just hungry. They don't run a five star resort here. I'm tempted to complain to the Empress." She went to move out of the doorway when Shilong pulled her back, and she turned to look at him.

His face was serious as he said, "You don't have to joke to hide your fear."

Alice physically flinched. No one had realised the joking was when she was the most afraid. She had picked up the trait from Hara and Gideon, who were at their worst when they were all in trouble.

Alice leaned forward and kissed him. He winced, but probably from his split lip. She apologised and pulled back and he shook his head. This wasn't the time for romantic interludes. She waved it off. They could discuss it later. Right then they had to avoid the Jade Guard and escape the palace.

She slipped her arm around his waist again to move further down the corridor. His healing must have been kicking in as he leaned on her less. They came out into a courtyard.

"You think you can turn into a dragon and get us out of here?" asked Alice.

His hand went up to the metal ring around his throat. "I can't at the moment."

Alice glanced at the necklace. It was decorated with small tiles of ebony, quartz and what appeared to be bone or ivory; the three things Hara had utterly forbidden from the ship. Alice wasn't surprised the dragons would first make another dragon weak by preventing him from changing.

She asked, "How'd you get the clothes, then?"

"A trick. I always keep a few things in a place that I can access even when my body is trapped, and moving things is only sticky, not impossible." She was glad she didn't have to help a naked man through the summer palace in the middle of Yeijing.

Before Alice could decide on the direction they would take out of the courtyard, Angel and Shishi came running in, Angel holding on with her wings spread out. Alice sighed with relief, but it was short-lived. Another man who appeared familiar and a woman Alice had never seen before ran into the courtyard. Alice worried that Shishi had led the enemy towards them.

Shilong said, "Harlen?"

Alice recognised the name. This was Gideon's brother. Alice had heard he had recently married, so the woman behind him was probably his mate.

Harlen growled. "I hope you haven't hurt my brother."

The woman said, "We don't have time for this. We have soldiers behind us and I have no idea where we are."

Harlen said, "I do."

Just as Shilong said, "I know."

Alice said, "Perfect, then lead the way out, and if you have a flare to send up to signal the Blazing Blunderbuss that would be excellent."

Harlen tilted his head up and spat out a large fireball. Alice hadn't realised they could do that while they were in human form. Certainly, Gideon hadn't done anything like that, but then they did live on an extremely flammable airship.

Lala smacked Harlen's arm. "Why did you do that? Now the soldiers will know where we are." She frowned at him. "You just want a bloody fight. No wonder they don't like it when you visit. You could always change into a dragon and take us with you."

Harlen said, "It will take longer with that thing here." He motioned to the necklace around Shilong's neck. "They'll be here before I can finish my change."

The woman came over to them. "I'm Lala, and it looks like we'll be taking a stand here until your ship comes to rescue us. Do either of you require a weapon?"

A strange request, but Alice would be pleased to have something to use if they were going to be overrun by soldiers. She nodded her head. Shilong materialised a long blade, obviously another one of those things that he could still retrieve despite not being able to change into a dragon.

Lala looked Alice over. "Something substantial, I think." She said to Harlen, "A baton, please."

Harlen looked Alice up and down. "I agree. She's a strong woman."

Lala said, "What flattery, Harlen. I would think you actually liked this woman."

Harlen's response was to materialise a baton and to say, "She's part of Hara's crew."

Lala chuckled and confessed to Alice, "He likes Hara but isn't very comfortable with it."

Lala grabbed the baton from Harlen and passed it to Alice. "Just swing like it's a hammer and with as much force as possible."

Lala demonstrated for Alice and Alice gave a few swings. Lala nodded, pleased. Any other instruction had to wait as soldiers and foo-lions poured into the courtyard.

They were only a small group against what appeared to be a flood. There was no way they would be able to keep them off, especially as Alice recognised the Jade Guard uniform.

Shishi jumped in front of them and hissed at the other foo-lions, who hissed back and shocked everyone by turning on the Jade Guards. Alice knew they weren't very effective except as guard dogs, but they would be able to distract the enemy so their small team could fight with more even odds.

Several of the soldiers managed to push past the foo-lions.

Lala said, "Remember, it will be a political nightmare if you kill people." Harlen just grunted.

Harlen charged, and with two large clubs appearing in his hands he attacked the closest Jade Guard. The foo-lions distracted the other guards but the normal human soldiers were left unharried, and with a cry they attacked.

Alice focused on the first man and swung her baton. He grunted when she hit him in the shoulder. She could hear the crunch of something and she hoped she hadn't done permanent damage.

Other soldiers attacked and Alice worked furiously, swinging the baton from side to side. She managed to keep them off her but she could feel the ache in her arm. There was only so long she could keep this up.

Alice risked a look at the others. Shilong was sweating and several of his wounds were bleeding again, as his clothes were stained. He seemed otherwise unhurt by the soldiers. She could see he would tire as she would.

Lala, on the other hand, had moved to another spot in the courtyard, as there had been too many unconscious men at her feet for her to easily move.

Harlen stood at her back and the two of them fought with the Jade Guards. The foo-lions, now mostly decimated, limped around or lay still on the ground.

Shishi appeared fine as Angel was flying around over his head and spitting needles at anyone who would approach. Angel only had a limited amount of needles. There was no way they would survive uncaptured until the Blazing Blunderbuss arrived. There was also a good chance that when it approached the military would be alerted, and they would have to face the whole of the Han army.

Alice didn't see the soldier who hit her, but the blow was only glancing as he had been in an awkward position. It did make her flinch back. Her arm was numb with the blow for a moment, but a moment long enough for her to drop her baton. Seeing she was unarmed, the other men didn't hesitate, and five closed in on her at the same time. She might have had a chance against them if they had just attacked her one at a time.

A loud crack filled the courtyard. Alice didn't see what it was at first as the soldiers tackled her to the ground. Their combined weight pushed the air out of her lungs.

A boom filled the air and the ground shook under them. Alice recognised the sensation. That was one of the Blazing Blunderbuss' bombs. They must be close for the ground to shake like that.

Alice was able to breathe as suddenly one of the soldiers was pulled off her. Bucking, she managed to free her arm. She rammed her elbow back and the soldier on top of her grunted as she hit him in his ribs. He was yanked off her back and Alice rolled over to see Shilong was throwing the soldier across the courtyard.

There was considerably more chaos than before. One of the roofs to the east was on fire and smoke filled the courtyard. There were two rings of fighters. One was around Harlen and Lala, who had moved once again to avoid tripping over unconscious forms. The other ring of soldiers was around the monkey man, Sun Wukong.

He had wings on his back held in tight. He used a staff and kept the others busy. He fought much like Shilong did. He flowed across the ground and threw his opponents around the courtyard.

A shadow made Alice look up. It was the Blazing Blunderbuss. They had to board soon or they would never leave the palace. Alice had an inkling of hope that they would get out of this when she heard the stomp of soldiers in marching uniform. That many soldiers would be impossible for them to fight.

Xu appeared in the archway leading into the courtyard. He studied Shilong. He then grimaced and did a strange thing. He put his hand on a pillar and made it disappear.

There was an awful crack and half the wall fell down. In a cloud of dust, Xu disappeared from sight.

Alice didn't quite understand what had happened but she could no longer hear the beat of soldiers' boots.

Shilong pulled Alice to her feet and held her against his side. She could feel the blood soaking his clothes.

Hermia would be on the Blazing Blunderbuss but she hoped they wouldn't need her skills. Gideon seemed to heal easily from wounds, even ones as extensive as Shilong's.

Wukong stopped in front of them. "You should leave."

Shilong said, "I can't. There's still too much to do."

"If the dragons would just leave us alone. This planet was ours first," Wukong growled out in his enhanced voice.

Alice added, "They aren't all bad. You must believe that or you wouldn't have helped us."

"You're all an agent for chaos. Don't mistake using you for helping you." With those words he gazed up, spun his staff and leaped out of the courtyard and over the fire that burned above their heads.

Harlen and Lala came up to them.

Lala said, "Get ready."

Alice took a moment too long to figure out what she meant. Harlen changed and Alice didn't have time to cover her eyes and she was blinded for a moment.

Harlen placed Lala on his back. Angel swooped up to Lala's shoulder and Shishi scrambled up to sit in front of her. Harlen grumbled and Lala patted his back.

Harlen caught Alice and Shilong in his claws.

Alice asked, "What about Xu?"

Before Shilong could answer they were pulled up as Harlen jumped into the air.

The Blazing Blunderbuss had moved away from the palace. There were no other airships in the air around them though. Most of them would avoid the fire, but Alice had expected to see at least the military—but they sat still on the other side of the city. Maybe Xu's people had made their move, and that was why the military stayed neutral.

Harlen dumped them on the deck.

Alice said to Lala, "Look after Shilong." Her words were redundant as Hermia rushed towards them. As the ship's doctor, Hermia would make sure Shilong was treated.

Alice ran onto the bridge. Susan and Murphy were having an argument.

Murphy indicated the weapons console. "Just one more. Surely one more won't get us into trouble."

Alice ignored Murphy and went to Susan, who was at the helm. Alice asked, "What excuse did you guys use to move the ship?"

Susan glared at Murphy one more time before she turned to Alice. "We told them we were testing a new engine and weren't sure it wouldn't blow up."

"Excellent. Take the Blazing Blunderbuss out of the city and swing wide and go back to port."

Susan gaped at her. "Are you nuts? They'll shoot us out of the sky the moment we approach those military ships."

Murphy said, "I'll shoot first."

Alice waved a hand at Murphy to silence him. "Just do it, Susan. Shilong was injured and I need to know I can depend on you."

Susan said, "I'll do it but I think they'll just blow us up."

Alice pointed out towards the military and the port where they had recently been tied up. "They can see what we're doing but they're playing blind and dumb. They'll pretend it wasn't us when we return, but we need to make it possible for them to say they didn't recognise us if they're ever questioned." She patted Susan reassuringly on her shoulder and went looking for Shilong.

Hermia had taken him to his room. Harlen and Lala were at the door.

Alice said, "Let me show you to a room. We're circling the city and we'll return some time tonight. We'll need to make plans, but not now."

Alice looked at Shilong and Lala nodded her head. "We'll be fine." Alice showed them to a door and left them before even showing them the room. If Harlen was like any other dragon, Alice knew he would happily make himself at home.

Hermia had Shilong undressed and laid out on the bed with blankets modestly covering him. Most of the wounds were crusted with scabs. Hermia was cleaning the skin with what seemed like vinegar. Hermia would be using something stronger but Alice would trust the young noblewoman's judgement.

Alice sat on the bed at Shilong's feet. She placed a hand on his foot, scared to touch him anywhere else in case it hurt him.

Alice asked, "Will he be alright?"

Hermia answered, "He's already healing. With some rest he'll be completely fine. Liam took the collar thing off him and he seemed to heal a lot better after that."

Alice watched fretfully while Hermia worked. Hermia pulled a blanket over Shilong, who was asleep, and pulled Alice away from the bed to the door of the room. Alice worried that Hermia intended to tell her that there was something very wrong. Instead, Hermia asked, "Did you find the captain and Gideon?"

"No, but I think the Jade Guard might have them. They waited for an opportunity to take me and Shilong. One of the rebels even came to our rescue. I don't know if he made it out. He collapsed part of the palace so we could get out. If they were behind the captain and Gideon being kidnapped, they would've allowed us to be taken by the Jade Guard."

Alice hesitated. She almost asked the others to go back for Xu, but as a dragon he could handle himself. She didn't like leaving any one behind.

9

Gideon heard water dripping in the distance. He hoped it was water, as there was a suspicious pain in his wing joint and he feared it might be his own blood dripping. He wasn't sure when he had changed into a dragon from his human form. He had spent a long while between consciousness and unconsciousness, so he wasn't sure exactly what happened. The last clear memory he had was questioning a woman in a market. After that his memories were murky with pain.

He remembered voices and a significant amount of agony. He wasn't surprised by the pain. It was what he had expected when he had been captured. He had also expected them to question him, but they hadn't. Even if they had asked him anything he doubted he would have been coherent.

The pain was a sharp point and it allowed Gideon to focus on what was around him. It was water, thankfully, as it seemed they were underground and water dripped off the walls.

The pain was because they had driven a large steel rod through his wing and then attached it to a ring submerged in rock. Dragons were good at manipulating atoms, except for three things to which they had to become vulnerable in order to travel to this world.

The ring was embedded in a large piece of quartz, one of the elements dragons couldn't manipulate very well. Maybe the Empress had been justified in worrying about someone bringing rampion to the planet if they had the skills to work the atoms of quartz when it was sticky to most dragons.

Gideon could likely have unglued the ring if he hadn't been in so much pain.

A door opened somewhere and a dragon in the shape of a man stood in front of Gideon. He was dressed in a uniform, so it was likely he was one of the Empress's men. He stood calmly with his hands behind his back in a casual military stance. When he spoke, it was clear he wasn't sure if Gideon was lucid or not.

"When we came here, we had so much hope."

Gideon growled.

The dragon said, "Ah, you can understand me. For a while there you were delirious."

Gideon tried to move but the awkward placement of the steel rod made it difficult. All he wanted was a claw free and he would crush the human-shaped dragon. His claws remained pinned under his body as pain raced through him from his pierced wing.

The human-shaped dragon said, "Tut, tut, you know better than to try to move. Settle, and we might even be able to have a conversation."

Gideon huffed out some hot air, reminding the other dragon he wasn't completely crippled, and that he could still cover the man with fire. As the man was also a dragon, he would be able to heal from any kind of burn injury, so attacking him would only be an annoyance, but it would probably make him feel better.

The Jade Guard soldier wasn't intimidated at all and chuckled, "I'm Enlai. The head of the Jade Guard. I have served my Empress faithfully for centuries. Even before we made this land our own. It should have been me the Empress called for when she rose to mate. Instead, she refuses to fly. You, lost prince, are going to change that. You're going to attack the Empress and force her into flight. That will be the signal to the others to fly. Of course, I will outstrip them and then I will be the emperor."

Gideon couldn't speak in any human language while he was in a dragon form, but the man in front of him would understand the grunts and growls that his dragon throat could manage.

"You're a fool, Enlai. A mating must be of mutual consent," Gideon growled.

Enlai waved that off. "That might have been true on our planet, but the rules have changed. The Empress must mate or the dragon race will be extinct in a matter of years."

"We can mate with humans. We don't need female dragons. They're difficult anyway. Humans are a much better choice for a mate. Trust me."

"You're a fool, lost prince."

Gideon was never accused of being a stupid man. Annoying, arrogant, and silly, but never stupid.

Enlai kept calling him a lost prince, just like the invitation had. Gideon asked, "Is it you I can thank for the invitation to Yeijing?"

"Ah, yes. The Empress doesn't care for her kingdom outside of the palace. She didn't even know you were in the area. It wasn't hard to forge an invite. After all, I do everything else," Enlai drawled smugly.

"So the Empress was just telling stories about the poisoner?"

Enlai laughed. "Oh, she thinks there was an attempt. She was never a bright one. Why do you think she came here? She was no one on our planet. Here she could have a collection and anything she wanted. She is happy sitting in her palace. She doesn't fly at all. What an abysmal life she leads. I will show her what it means to be a true dragon, and I'll bring her to heel. Female dragons are so inferior to male dragons."

Gideon laid his head on the ground, his snout not far from Enlai. "So you want me to force the Empress to fly, to mate."

"I don't care if she wants to mate. She just needs to fly. The men are so set to mate that they will assume she is mating even if she doesn't call."

Gideon was disgusted. It was a wholesale rape of the Empress by whatever dragon caught up to her. Since she hadn't flown in over a millennium, he doubted the Empress could fly at all. It would not take much for her to be caught and taken by one of the male dragons.

Gideon tilted his head to one side so one eye looked directly at Enlai. "What makes you think I'll cooperate with any of this?"

Before Enlai answered Gideon could hear Hara swear and grunt in pain. Chains rattled and Hara was thrown down in front of Enlai and Gideon.

Gideon growled. "Let her go."

"Only if you help us," Enlai said fiercely.

"You're a fool, Enlai." Only a fool would threaten anything in his collection. Gideon wasn't just his brother's sibling; he was a power to fear in his own right.

Hara came up swinging, but the chains around her waist and wrists made her slow and the Jade Guards who had brought her in easily stepped away from her feeble attacks.

She growled at them, "Come closer, you worms. I'll gut you if you just kept still."

Gideon blew some hot air in her direction and she turned, ready to attack him. She stopped and said in a soft, pained voice, "Gideon?"

Rushing up to him, she pressed herself against his snout. He kept still as she sobbed against his scales.

Enlai drawled, "How sweet, it seems your mate missed you."

"You'll burn in hell, Enlai," Gideon growled.

"Maybe, but not for a very long time." Enlai motioned to his men and they dragged Hara back and attached her chains to a ring in the wall. Enlai tipped a hand to his head in a mock salute and left the room with his men.

Hara said, "I want to skin him alive. Slowly. Very slowly." Her hands shaped into claws as if she wanted to skin him with her bare hands.

Gideon grunted his approval. He turned to Hara. She would have only understood half of the conversation. Maybe that was why the guards felt brave enough to leave her here with him.

Hara said, "They're fools to leave me here to plot with you. Do you know what they want from us?"

Gideon clicked his teeth in a code he and Angel were developing in order for her to communicate better.

Hara hissed. "That's despicable. Are you going to go along? And before you answer, you don't need to worry about me. When they leave me alone, I'll get out. They left my hair up." Her voice was tinged with smugness.

Gideon huffed out hot air in amusement. They had underestimated his mate. Most did.

Alice was exhausted. She had sent the others to get some rest as she brought the Blazing Blunderbuss back into its berth. There was no fanfare from the other ships next to them. Harlen had agreed with her that the military were staying out of the whole affair on purpose, so there was little risk in returning to the city and to their spot among the highly armed ships.

The ship dipped suddenly and Alice's heart leapt. The ship did that whenever Gideon pulled himself on board. When she turned around, Xu entered the bridge. He wore his dusty uniform from before.

He looked her over. "Is Shilong here?"

Alice nodded and motioned for him to follow her. She took him to Shilong's room.

Hermia dozed in the chair next to the bed and woke when the door opened. She blinked at the two of them, then muttered something before she excused herself and left the room.

Xu asked, "Was it that bad?"

"Probably not, but it wasn't a walk in the park." Alice looked Xu over. He still sported some bruises, so she wondered if he was hiding injuries. She said, "Thank you for what you did. Did the others suspect that you had blocked the way?"

"No. They only just dug me out, and they were fuming over your escape in some unknown vessel. They seem to be chasing their tails. Enlai is playing a deep game and that makes me uncomfortable."

"Yeah, things seem a little more than complicated. We do appreciate that you managed to get the military to stay out of this."

Xu shook his head. "It wasn't my doing. I was at the palace when I found out that you two had been taken. I hadn't even told the others when the commotion started. There are several stories going around the palace. Some say that the Wyvern Empire sent assassins, while others suggest that the foo-lions went crazy and started attacking everyone."

Alice shrugged. "The confusion helps us in the meantime. If you weren't the one to put the military on hiatus then we have another motive behind their move, and that makes me nervous."

Xu bowed his head, acknowledging this. He motioned to Shilong still asleep in his bed. "You can count on me to help, though it might not be in the way you expect. Have you any idea of where your captain is?"

"The Jade Guard, probably. I haven't debriefed Angel yet."

Xu frowned, and Alice sighed as she prepared to explain the clockwork dragon. "Angel, a clockwork creature that belongs to Hara, went with Hara last night, but now the two of them are here via the summer palace, where they helped me escape. Angel and Gideon have been working on a code so they can speak. It's written down somewhere, but it'll take a while to decipher what she's able to tell us. I have a fair clue she'll tell us that it was the Jade Guard who took Hara, as it seems Enlai is up to something."

Xu studied her for a long moment then said, "You're different from the women here."

Startled, Alice said, "Oh, and why's that?"

"You are not as—" He was at a loss for words, so Alice sarcastically helped him out. "Subservient? Browbeaten? You can't expect your women to flourish if you refuse to let them grow in the first place."

"It's unnatural to teach women; they might get ideas."

Alice snorted. This wasn't the first time she had come across this kind of sentiment, and she had also seen it in her own country.

Her father had been the one in her family who had encouraged her to learn. He had wanted a son, and when he only had daughters, he had taken that as a challenge. Out of all the sisters, Alice was the only one who had taken to the books, while the others had developed other skills. Her father had stunned everyone when he celebrated all his daughters equally. The men in her town had ridiculed her father for his attitude.

Alice tapped Xu's chest. "What you consider unnatural is actually the true order of things. You should learn to see things clearer or it might all come to bite you in your ass."

Shilong shifted in his sleep, and Alice pulled Xu away from the door. She closed it quietly and said in a softer tone, "What are your plans now?"

"I'll return to my post. I need to be in play to make the most difference."

Alice nodded. She wasn't sure what Xu wanted out of all this chaos, but she wouldn't begrudge him wanting to play a part.

"When the fun starts to happen, you'll know where to find us," she said.

"You'll go for your captain then?" Xu asked, but the question was rhetorical.

"We'll do it with a bang."

Xu's eyes sparked with delight and he said fiercely, "I hope so."

He bowed politely to her and left. Alice hoped she could deliver on her promise, or none of them would be getting out of Han.

Everyone seemed to migrate to the mess hall in the morning. Angel chittered away in her code and got frustrated when Alice didn't translate her chattering fast enough.

Harlen asked, "Does she know where they are?"

"No, but she knows it was the Jade Guard. She saw the uniform. Apparently, they're not afraid of reprisals. Or they think they'll play their hand before we come after them."

Lala said, "It's more likely they have underestimated us."

Alice looked up Lala. She had seen her fight. The woman was not soft, but she was so tiny that it always amazed Alice when she thought back to their escape from the palace.

Alice was distracted when Liam came in. He sat down with a sigh and Alice asked, "Everything alright?"

He nodded. "Those soldiers are like four-year-olds on sugar."

Alice puckered her brow. She hadn't been aware there had been any soldiers on the Blazing Blunderbuss.

He noticed the frown and explained. "Several Han soldiers came over to inspect the ship this morning. You all were still asleep so I took them around. They had heard there was a mess at the palace, and some were nervous that we might have had something to do with it, so they wanted to make sure we really had been testing out our new engine."

Alice's heart dropped, but since Liam seemed calm she kept her voice calm as she asked, "We don't have a new engine, do we?"

"Oh no, but the one we have is so massively advanced that they were drooling over it." Liam got animated as he started to talk about the engine. "We found the gas that helps us float can also be used as fuel, but making the gas on the fly is a bit difficult. Hara figured out how to do that and now we mostly run on water."

Alice asked, confused, "Water? Seriously?"

"Yeah, it's easier to come by, but heavier than the coal we usually use. So even though it's better, we don't have all the power we could have if we dumped the weight."

Alice decided the conversation wasn't important to their situation and waved Liam off. "Did the soldiers leave?"

"Eventually. They wanted to take the engine apart and make sketches. Hara wouldn't be pleased with that, so I stalled and told them to come back once we had finished testing it. I assumed you wanted to move the ship again without suspicion? Well, I told them we would need to go out again."

Alice sighed with relief. "Thank you, Liam, that does make things easier."

Everyone looked at Shilong when he entered. He appeared a sight better than he had the day before. It was amazing what healing the dragons could perform. It was a wonder humans had managed to kill any at all.

He sat down. "What news is there of Gideon and the captain?"

"None so far, but Angel here says it was the Jade Guard," Alice filled him in.

Harlen said, "I'll go for my brother."

Alice nodded. "So will we. Liam, Susan, and Murphy will stay here with the ship and give us cover when we need it. Where's Talen, by the way?"

Murphy said, "Gone."

Alice pondered. "You mean he went out by himself? We warned him that was dangerous."

Murphy added, "He took all his things with him as well."

There was a tense silence and no one wanted to fill it.

After a long pause Alice said, "The rest of us will go to the headquarters of the Jade Guard."

She looked at Shilong, who said, "That is in one of those towers they use to watch for the Empress."

"We'll go there and look for the captain. At the very least we should find someone who'll know where they are."

Harlen agreed, and Lala said, "The Jade Guard is mostly made up of dragons."

And yet a few days previously Harlen and Lala had been able to defeat over two dozen of them by themselves. Lala continued with a tilt of her head as she thought. "If we attack while they're inside the building they're unlikely to transform. Also, I have a few gadgets that can make it sticky for anyone there to pull any tricks."

Shilong asked, "Who are you?"

Lala smiled, not in the least offended by his tone, and offered her hand to him. "I'm Lala, dragon hunter and Harlen's mate."

Shilong had started to reach out to take her hand, and it was clear he was trying to embrace Western culture, but when he heard Lala was a dragon hunter his hand stopped in midair and his mouth gaped.

Alice asked what seemed to be stuck in his throat, "A dragon hunter?"

Harlen said, "She is mine."

Alice glanced at Harlen, surprised by the fierce tone of his voice.

Lala sighed. "Yes, but I'm also mine. Don't worry, Shilong, I'm not going to go homicidal and kill you in your sleep."

Harlen snorted and Lala glared at him, but there was warmth in her eyes. Alice decided to get the conversation back on track. "Xu says he'll help us and I still want to talk to Sun Wukong. I think he can help us."

Shilong said, "We have been looking for him and there has not been any clue to his identity."

Liam added, "He found Gideon and Hara when he wanted to speak to them. Maybe he'll find you when you go visit the Jade Guard."

Alice chewed on her lip as she thought. "I hope so."

———————————

There was a lot to do before they could find Hara and Gideon. Lala was working with Liam to make some weapons that would slow the dragons down, and Shilong was on the ground at a telegram outpost sending a message to the rebels. Hopefully they could at the very least cause a distraction.

Alice was on the deck moving things so when they had to go into battle, they wouldn't dislodge anything and destabilize the Blazing Blunderbuss.

She turned and jumped back and whacked herself into a crate. She swore softly. "You could've knocked."

Sun Wukong didn't say anything. Alice sighed. "What are you doing here?"

Though she was glad he was there. They could do with his help.

"You destroyed part of the summer palace."

"Yes, you were there for that part, remember?" Alice reminded him.

He shook his head. "I've been fighting here for years and I've not even dented a foo-lion. You're here for a few weeks and already you have destroyed a wing in the summer palace."

"Destruction isn't really why we're here." He had spoken about how they were agents of chaos in the palace, and she winced when she realised he was right.

He waved that off. "What are your plans?"

Alice smiled. "Funny you should ask. We're planning to go to the Jade Guard tower and ask some questions. Very forcefully. You see, it was them who took our captain and Gideon."

"I'm not surprised. They have run amok for years. The Empress doesn't care what they do."

"Not all dragons are evil."

His snort was more animal than human through the contraption that distorted his voice. "If your dragons are the only examples of decent dragons, then I don't think there will be a time when the Hans will deal with the Han dragons."

Sadly, she thought he might be right, but hopefully they could leave the country in a better state than the one in which they had found it.

Curious, Alice asked, "Do we have you to thank for the convenient blindness of the soldiers?"

"You could say that. The military have been encouraged for a long time to turn their eyes away from what the dragons are doing, and that was none of our doing. All I had to do was remind them of that fact."

So the neglect over the years had made it easy for them to ignore that parts of the summer palace had gone up in smoke the day before.

Lala and Harlen arrived on the deck. They saw Sun Wukong and Harlen bowed his head to the dressed-up human. Alice could tell the man was disconcerted by the respect shown by the dragon. Maybe they could convince him to treat with the dragons after all.

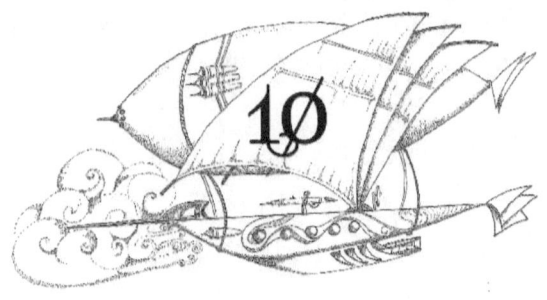

The five of them approached the tower without any interference from guards.

Lala said suspiciously, "There aren't many people around. If they were keeping prisoners, unquestionably they would at least have lookouts and guards."

"They mightn't be keeping Hara and Gideon here, but someone here will know where they are," Alice said. Harlen growled but didn't add anything to the conversation.

When they entered, a dragon arose from a desk. "You aren't supposed to be here." Since he spoke in Imperial it was clear he knew exactly who they were.

They ignored him and he picked up a bell that was on his desk and started ringing it. Harlen threw something and the dragon yelped as a blade buried in the hand holding the bell. He dropped the bell and backpedalled out of the room. He went through the only other door, which led to stairs that would go up the tower.

They followed him up the stairs. Lala put her hand on Harlen's arm. "Let me go first."

He nodded his head to her and she took the lead. Shilong asked, "A woman?"

Harlen said, "She is a dragon hunter. She has abilities even I do not possess."

Alice was amused. "Jealous a little bit there, Harlen?"

His answer was a simple, "Yes."

Wukong said, "I've never heard of a dragon ever being jealous of a human before."

Harlen turned to look at Wukong. "There are many things about the humans that make you an interesting breed. Do not let the fools here make you believe all dragons do not appreciate humans."

Lala said, "That's a speech from Harlen, so he must feel strongly on it."

The rooms all the way up the tower were empty of dragons. Alice predicted they would go to the top where the Jade Guard could transform to dragon form, except she realised they hadn't thought it through very well. The top floor was open but cramped, and it could only accommodate one dragon at a time. They would still have to fight as humans.

Alice had raided Hara's room for some of her gadgets and Lala had given her some more. Alice would make sure that at least one of the dragons was in a state to answer their questions.

When they reached the top of the stairs, Harlen said, "Where's my brother?" There were several dragons in human form with weapons already in their hands.

One of the dragons growled back, "He's a traitor."

"He's the one that brought you here to this planet. Your loyalty should be to him first. If anyone is a traitor, it is you." But it was clear Harlen was finished trying to negotiate. He drew a large axe from nowhere. "Traitors lose their heads."

Alice knew they didn't intend to kill any of the dragons, so she had to assume the axe was merely to intimidate. Then she saw Harlen swing it, and he wasn't pulling his punches. The axe buried into the arm of the

129

dragon and he screamed in pain. Harlen kicked him off the axe but didn't go in to finish him. Harlen and the others wanted to put the dragons out of action for a while, unlike back at the summer palace where all they had intended was to put them out long enough to escape.

Lala dropped a dragon in front of Alice. "He knows something." She then returned to the melee.

Alice crouched down. The dragon was bleeding and one of his eyes was burst. He still managed to glare at her. Alice tilted her head because she knew that was a gesture the dragon would understand. She placed her arm on her knee. "I'm not a dragon, but I've been around enough of you to know just how far I can take you before you'll die."

She didn't, but she was taking a page out of Harlen's book. She pulled out a knife Hara had given her a long time ago for her to defend herself.

It seemed a lifetime ago from the naïve girl that Alice had been to this ex-pirate first mate that she had transformed into.

Alice glanced up to see Shilong fighting. He was mainly throwing his opponents, and he didn't care if it was off the tower completely. He had such agile moves that appeared more fluid than violent. Alice leaned down on the dragon's wounded shoulder and the man yelled. "Now you'll tell us where our people are and we'll leave you alive," she said. "The others won't need to know that you said anything."

He stared at her, and Alice could tell why Lala had picked this one rather than others. There was hesitation in his eye.

Alice leaned closer. "They're in our collection. You might have forgotten what it means to be in a collection, but we haven't."

"You aren't a dragon, you don't know what collections mean," he said fiercely.

Alice said in an interested tone, "I know you protect your collections, and I know that you have the choice whether you stay in a collection or not. If you don't think your Empress has protected you and appreciated you, surely it's time to find another collection that will."

Remembering the way Enlai had ordered his men around as if they were merely extensions of himself, Alice added, "You're an individual in a collection but you do make up a greater whole together. What kind of collection are you part of?"

He grunted, his green eye sharp with his pain and indecision. Eventually he said, "Your people aren't in my collection."

Alice worried he wouldn't tell them anything but he continued, "We have a temple that's ours. On the edge of the city. We take people there who have been difficult."

She was sure she could get better directions from Shilong or Wukong, who knew the city better. Alice nodded her head in thanks and stood up, then whistled as their prearranged signal.

Shilong turned to look at her and transformed, shoving several more dragons off the tower. He grabbed her and leaped off the tower. He put her up behind his neck and she wrapped her hands in the mane that flowed from his head.

He was different from other dragons she had seen as he was a bright emerald green. He was also longer and more sinuous than the Wyvern empire dragons.

They had left the dragons in the tower injured but still alive. It would take them a while to recover, but no permanent damage had been dealt so Alice didn't expect a pursuit. When she looked behind her, she could see Wukong in the air and Harlen as a large golden dragon still in the tower.

The Blazing Blunderbuss was waiting for them, and Shilong lifted her onto the deck before he transformed. Lala jumped off Harlen's back and rolled onto the deck shortly after they had landed. Harlen changed just above the ship and caught himself on the ropes that dangled off the envelope above the airship. He swung himself over the deck and let go of the ropes. He landed in a crouch. "Where to next?"

"He said they take difficult people to a temple on the outskirts of the city," said Alice. She thought of those dragon priests she had seen at the Cuju game. She had gotten the impression then they were crowd control, and it would make sense that they had their own headquarters.

She looked at Shilong. Before he could answer, Wukong flew onto the deck and landed, his wings coming in tight against his back. Gears whirred and clicked as he settled on the deck.

Shilong said, "There is one temple dedicated to dragons on the outskirts of the city. I've never been there. I've never been comfortable with the way dragons are worshipped, and the humans they use as enforcers for their own people."

Wukong said, "I know of it as well. There are tunnels that lead underneath. It would be a good place to keep prisoners."

Harlen nodded. "Then we'll go there. Send this ship in the right direction and we'll drop in on them."

They took Hara away before they removed the steel rod from Gideon's wing. Free, Gideon changed back into his human shape. Pain went through his shoulder and he involuntarily cupped his shoulder with his other hand.

Enlai smirked. He likely thought he had teased Gideon with how close Hara had been, thinking they hadn't been able to communicate with Gideon in his dragon state. That was Enlai's mistake, but Gideon wouldn't enlighten the man yet.

Gideon dressed in the court uniform that Enlai had provided. He felt grimy, as Enlai hadn't bothered to provide a bath, and he said, "I feel like a beggar. Surely you could have at least provided a basin."

"Stop being a dandy."

"That's who I am."

Enlai snorted. "I heard of you back on our planet. You're far from pompous, so you can drop the act."

Gideon shrugged. Most took him for granted, even his brothers. Sometimes when his deeds were spread rather than his reputation, he got this reaction from others. It was disappointing, as he put a lot of effort into his dandy act.

Enlai said, "You're to meet with the Empress. She'll be expecting you. While you're there we'll make it appear like the rebels are attacking the palace. You are to convince her to flee the palace or she'll be killed by the rebels. If not, you'll attack her yourself and force her to take to the air."

Gideon could see several flaws in this plan but didn't point them out to Enlai. Instead, he just nodded his head. He would go along with it as Hara would need time to escape, and he was hoping that when Enlai took him to the palace most of them would come with him, leaving Hara fewer people to avoid.

Gideon brushed down his clothes. "Let us get this disaster over with."

Enlai caught his arm before he could lead the way out of the room. "We have your mate, and I don't have to adhere to rules. You would not want a creature that no longer has her limbs."

Gideon hissed, "If you touch her, I'll pull your head off."

Enlai snorted. "You're a scholar. You're not a warrior."

Gideon raised an eyebrow. "I'm a dragon with a collection."

Enlai just glowered, and Gideon started to gather that the idea of collections had been perverted in this country by the Empress, a perversion that had been perpetuated by her people like Enlai. No wonder things were not as they were supposed to be.

As they left the building, Gideon hoped Hara was alright.

<hr />

The airship dipped and Xu pulled himself onto the deck. Alice was with the others, and they were readying themselves to go down to the temple to rescue Hara and Gideon.

He looked them over. "Have you found out where your crew is?"

Harlen grunted. Obviously he didn't want to share information with the rebel dragon, though he had been happily sharing information with Sun Wukong.

Shilong said, "They're keeping them in the temple where they worship the Jade Guard."

Xu snorted as if that should have been the obvious answer. Shilong asked, "Will you join us?"

Xu's hesitation was more than enough of an answer, but he added, "The Jade Guard will be busy with you and they'll not be guarding the Empress. We'll deal with her."

Alice snapped. "Are you crazy?"

Xu looked at her, surprised that a woman would speak to him that way, but Alice wasn't intimidated by the look.

"By 'deal,' I gather you either mean to force her to mate or you'll kill her." Alice didn't think what the Empress was doing was right, but that didn't give anyone the right to force her to mate.

"We would never kill the Empress," Xu said icily.

Alice shook her head. Couldn't these people see how wrong it was to force the Empress into any coupling? Alice agreed that the Empress should have mated a long time ago, but these dragons didn't have the right to force her to do anything.

Wukong said, "You see?"

Alice turned to the man dressed in a mechanical monkey suit and raised an eyebrow. "You don't have a moral leg to stand on either, monkey man. You hide behind a mask, so you don't have to worry about the consequences of your actions. You should be standing up to the dragons and telling them that this is your world and they're invaders and they need to learn how to share. You included. Killing dragons in a wholesale way isn't going to free Han; it will only make it less."

Alice threw her hands up in the air. "I'm tired of arguing. We need to get our people back because they're in our collection and they're family."

Harlen came up to Xu. "Go about your plans."

He then shoved Xu off the deck. Xu changed as he fell, so there was no harm, but it was clear Harlen wasn't pleased with the rebel's plans either.

* * *

Enlai escorted Gideon to the island where the Empress resided. Gideon felt like a prisoner although his guard had no weapon and Gideon wasn't tied up. There was no way Enlai would let him go anywhere except to confront the Empress.

Stopping outside of the pavilion, Gideon said to Enlai, "There'll be no convincing her that she's in danger if her fierce protector is standing there by her side."

Enlai hesitated. Gideon had wondered if he had expected to watch the whole thing and get an advantage when the Empress rose to fly.

He patted Enlai on the shoulder. "You have to trust me. I'll get the Empress out of this palace one way or another. You have my mate, after all." Hara had probably already escaped.

Gideon already knew what he intended do with the Empress, but he doubted Enlai would be pleased with the results. Gideon flashed the Jade Guard a grin. Enlai scowled but motioned for Gideon to enter the pavilion. His hesitation made Gideon think his captor was starting to see that his plan was falling apart.

Gideon found the Empress lying in the sun of a courtyard. She raised her head when he entered and blew hot air in his direction.

She said, "I thought you were lost again. Your brother was here the other day making a mess again. Can he even live in a building? Because every time he comes here, he seems to destroy part of my home."

"Harlen has very little regard for belongings that people don't care for. When was the last time you saw the rest of your palace outside of this pavilion?"

"It's comfortable here," The Empress said, too casually. It was clear she didn't take any of this seriously.

"That's an excuse and you know it."

The Empress huffed again. She said conversationally, "My astronomers told me something interesting today. They told me last night several stars disappeared out of the sky only to reappear nearly at dawn. There were no clouds last night, so they have no idea why the stars disappeared like that. To think, such large objects in the sky disappearing, and yet only my astronomers noticed."

Gideon didn't let her distract him. "I was sent here to manipulate you to do something that would be a bad idea for you and every dragon in this empire."

"Manipulate me?" she growled.

"Yes, by one of your so-called collection."

The Empress sounded bored as she said, "How dare they?"

"You already knew." It wasn't a question.

"I knew my time here was coming to an end. I made a mistake. I should have taken a page out of your brother's book and left the humans to rule. Instead, I followed the pattern of the Gregori brothers from Rosh."

Gideon said unhelpfully, "They're dead."

"Yes, and I should've remembered that. I knew leaving would throw Han into chaos." She waved a claw lazily as she spoke.

"Chaos is inevitable, as everything tends towards entropy." Gideon preferred to lean on science when things were frustrating.

The Empress waved an apathetic claw towards him. "I would disagree, but I have no idea what you just said."

"You should have kept up the advances. The humans make us extend our boundaries."

The Empress huffed. "Nonsense, we're superior in every way."

It was an opinion held by most dragons, though Gideon didn't agree with them. He knew there would be no way to convince the Empress that her thoughts were small-minded, especially since most dragons agreed with her. "The only way out, Empress, is to die."

"That's not acceptable." Her eyes snapped with the anger she managed to keep out of her voice.

"Not a real death. Just your identity. You can't be Empress anymore."

The Empress turned her head, so her eye was looking directly at him. "Tell me more."

There was a muffled boom in the distance. Gideon turned to look in the direction of the sound. He hadn't realized Enlai would make the rebel attack seem so real.

"Maybe we can discuss the details of my plan once we leave."

The Empress looked up at the sky. "I'm not a fan of flying. It requires so much work."

"Well, you aren't going to like it any more as a passenger. You need to change into a human."

The Empress went still at his suggestion. "And be so vulnerable? Never."

"If you fly out of here, Enlai has dragons waiting to mate with you. It has to be as a human that you leave."

"Fine." The Empress changed and stood as a naked woman in the courtyard. It seemed so much larger without the dragon dominating the space. She was a pleasant-looking woman, but there wasn't anything exceptional about her. Her hair, though, black as night and completely straight, almost touched the ground. She crossed her arms over her chest, impatient for things to move forward. Gideon changed into a dragon.

He didn't ask the Empress if she had any clothes, because she had been a dragon for a very long time and her attitude towards humans meant it was unlikely. He materialized a fur coat and wrapped her up.

There was another boom, this time much closer. Gideon didn't waste any time. He grabbed the Empress and leaped into the air.

A lice studied the foo-lions that stood guard
outside the temple. These were not clockwork
creatures, but bronze sculptures with a green
patina.

She said to Shilong, "They'd look almost cute if it
weren't for the fact they're guarding a prison instead of a
temple. I can see why the Empress made a bunch of
these to look after her palace."

"I don't think this place was ever used as a proper
temple. It was made by us to make people accept dragons
more. I never liked the idea of encouraging the masses
to worship us as anything other than creatures of flesh
and blood, no matter how advanced we are."

Alice saw the social expediency of convincing the
human race that dragons were gods. It left a bitter taste
in her mouth. She squinted at him. "Not superior?"

"No, I don't think we're superior." Alice warmed to
that comment. The dragons from the Wyvern Empire
were convinced they were superior to humans, even if
they believed humans had the right to rule their own
world.

Harlen pushed past them. "My brother is in there. We
don't have time to give puppy eyes to each other."

Lala followed him. "Don't mind him. He's mad at me because I don't love him yet." Lala didn't explain that cryptic comment.

Wukong stomped past them as well. He knew the interior of the temple and led the way. There was no one in the temple itself. No one was expecting them. There was no need to have guards when the place was supposed to be secret.

Wukong led them to a door at the back of the temple and through some smaller rooms. This led to stairs. These were guarded. Harlen blew some fire down the stairs and charged straight away. There was some screams.

Wukong asked, "Is he going to leave any of them for us?"

Lala said, "He's just angry. It's better he takes it out on these idiots."

She followed Harlen down the stairs. There were groaning men on the stairs with smouldering clothes. None seemed to be severely injured. Harlen was bent on speed rather than making sure the dragons couldn't attack him from behind, but then he did have a rear guard. Wukong applied his staff where it was needed to ensure the people stayed down.

At the bottom of the stairs there was a large chamber. There was a disturbing amount of blood on the ground. Harlen was crouched by the puddle. He said, "Dragon's."

Lala added, "In dragon form. This was just a small wound."

It didn't appear that way to Alice, but she would take the expert's opinion on it all. There were several doors leading off the large round chamber.

Alice asked, "How did they get a dragon into here?"

Lala pointed to a door and Alice squinted and saw that it was a smaller door placed into a larger door. It was clear this place was made for dragons.

Wukong said from one of the doorways, "This way. It's the only locked door in the place." He must have been exploring while they had been checking out the puddle of blood. They all followed Wukong.

Alice heard something scrape and she looked up to where she had heard it. The others passed her down the corridor. There was a grate in the ceiling where air from above would come down to the underground rooms.

The grate popped open and Hara's head appeared upside down. She grinned at them. "I thought I recognised the voices."

Hara's head disappeared and her legs dropped down. The others had stopped when they heard Hara's voice. Alice said, "We came to rescue you."

Hara dropped to the ground and dusted off her hands. "Excellent. We have to go. Enlai took Gideon to the palace to force the Empress to fly. We need to get to Shihua caves. That's where Gideon has taken the Empress."

Sun Wukong said, "The Empress is out of the city?"

"I see you're here helping." She waved to indicate his presence.

Wukong said, "Your people create chaos and that benefits my plans."

Hara raised an eyebrow. "All well and good, Mr monkey man, but we need to move. Enlai is going to realise his plans aren't working and Gideon is on his own."

Harlen said, "The Blazing Blunderbuss is waiting for our signal."

Hara clapped her hands in excitement. "Excellent. Now did Angel and her beau get away?"

Alice answered, "And saved us in the meantime."

Hara turned a sharp look to Alice and said practically, "We'll share stories later. Right now we have to rescue an Empress and save Han from a bloody civil war."

When they all turned, Wukong said, "I'll have to leave you."

Hara stopped and turned back to him. He added, "My people will never get a chance like this to take our country back from the dragons."

Alice said, "You could always work with the dragons."

"Never."

Hara said, "That's your choice, Sun Wukong. We won't help you murder dragons."

Wukong said fiercely, "At the moment self-defence is my only intent." He pushed past them and ran up the stairs.

Hara shook her head in disappointment. "People can justify murder with that argument."

Before they could go any further, Alice asked, "They didn't hurt you?"

"No, they were trying to convince Gideon to do something for them, so they were reasonably gentle with me. They even left me with my hair pins. What I didn't count on was having a cell with no key hole on my side." She motioned to the ceiling. "Luckily the vents weren't locked."

Alice wasn't surprised Hara had figured out a way to escape.

Gideon stood at the mouth of the cave. The sky was filled with the forms of green and white dragons. The Han dragons had seen the direction they had taken when they had left the palace but Gideon had confused them when they couldn't figure out if Gideon was escaping or not. He was out of sight by the time they had figured out that he had taken the Empress in human form. That gave him enough time to hide.

The Han dragons were now looking diligently for him and the Empress. They had figured out that because Hara and the rest were still in Yeijing he wouldn't go far, so they kept their search close to the city. Gideon turned when the Empress asked, "So how am I going to die?"

"When was the last time someone saw you in your human form?" She was a small woman who appeared to be middle-aged. When the Empress first travelled here, she would have chosen a form. It surprised him that she had picked a form that wasn't very Imperial.

"Over a thousand years. I don't like being human." He must have gathered that from watching her, as she kept tripping on things and she never knew where to put her hands.

"Well, you'll have to get used to it. Or you could leave Han." No one would be able to recognise her human form, no matter where she went, but if she wanted to fly as a dragon she would have to go to a place where there were no other dragons. There just weren't enough female dragons for her to be able to hide that way.

"No, Han is my home."

Gideon raised an eyebrow at the fierce tone of her voice. "Have you become attached to this world, by any chance?"

"It's better than our old world. There, everyone was ruled by such strict social structures." That was one of the best things about the human world, but he did find it ironic coming from the Empress.

"You do realise the irony in that. Han has stricter social structures and that's because of you." She waved a hand at the comment and stared at her hand for a long moment.

She was now dressed in some clothes that he had purchased for Hara but hadn't gotten around to giving her. The clothes were feminine and he had been waiting for a time when Hara had been feeling particularly amorous. With the baby coming he doubted that would be any time soon, so he could risk giving them to the Empress.

She almost appeared normal. If she didn't look so awkward in her skin, she could have passed as human.

"I'll tell the other dragons that to prevent a great injustice I hid you away. Of course, none of them will believe me, and they'll assume that I've killed you or sent you back to our home plane." Gideon fleshed out the plan. He knew Hara wasn't going to be pleased that he was adding another label to their group. The label of pirate had undoubtedly come with its own issues. They would now have to avoid other dragons once it was known they were dragon killers.

He sighed. Hara was right. They should have waited to have children. That was purely his fault as well. He would have to do some more grovelling for the next tragedy he planned to add to their lives.

Gideon turned back to the dragons flying in the sky. There was another group flying out from the city. They were in armour and they flew in formation. Gideon tilted his head as he watched. That must be the rebels.

The searching Jade Guard weren't paying attention to the sky at all and became aware of the rebels too late. They scrambled to gather together in defence but the rebels had already reached them, and picked off the first of the Jade Guards. Gideon winced as one of them had his wing torn off.

It appeared the rebels felt as he did; that no matter their differences, death was not the answer. But maiming apparently was still acceptable.

Without taking his eyes off the fight, Gideon said to the Empress, "I think it's time to leave."

He transformed and reached back into the cave to pick up the Empress. The rebels and the Jade Guards did not spot them as Gideon flew around the mountain. He didn't intend to go far. A little distance away he dropped to the ground and changed back into his human form.

The Empress shook her skirts. "An abysmal way to travel. Surely you could've let me fly."

Gideon simply said, "We couldn't risk it." He gestured for her to start walking.

"Where're we going?"

"There's a small village on the river. You'll be living there for a while. If you want to leave, you'll have to travel as a human, but I suggest you get to know people."

"Why? They're so boring."

Gideon thought "boring" was the life she had been living. "Humans can be interesting. I suggest finding one who's interesting."

He thought of Hara as he said this, but he brought his mind back to the Empress's problem. "At least a decade, I'd suggest. For us that's nothing. Just enjoy being different for a while. After a decade you can decide what you want to do."

The Empress huffed. "I hope you don't expect me to work."

"Probably, but it'll depend on the village and whether you have money."

She said stiffly, "I have money."

He grinned at her. "Then I suggest you set yourself up as a rich merchant in the village and you'll unlikely have to work. Life will be simple. You won't have the luxuries you had in the palace. You'll have to settle for linen instead of silk."

"What would I need silk for? The bloody material burns so easily."

Things would not be so awful for the Empress, as she had been living a simple life as a dragon. It took them an hour to walk the rest of the way to the village. Gideon hadn't wanted to land too close and have anyone associate the Empress with sightings of dragons.

The village wasn't large. He remembered it from their flight into the city. There were people in the shallows dredging the water with nets. Some saw them and yelled to others.

Gideon stopped. "This is where I'll leave you, Empress. May you have a good life."

"That's hardly possible, but at least it's a life." Gideon didn't want to argue, so he just bowed his head slightly to her.

People were coming up to them to see what they were about as he walked away. He wasn't sure the Empress would follow his instructions, but he also didn't think she was as dimwitted as Enlai had assumed. Considering Gideon didn't have a high opinion of Enlai's intelligence, he wasn't surprised the man had misjudged the Empress.

Hopefully by the time the Empress was bored with the village and the Han had gone back to a human government, she might have learned to love the people along with the country.

Gideon took a circuitous route back to the cave area. He landed on the top of a mountain and changed. Several of the dragons had seen him change and some came to the mountain. The fighting seemed to be suspended by mutual agreement while they talked to him.

Enlai and Xu were the two that approached him. Gideon took a seat on a rock and both Enlai and Xu glared at his casual nature.

Enlai growled out, "What've you done with the Empress? You were supposed to make her fly. I had everything planned. Surely you couldn't have messed it up so royally."

Gideon popped a small volcanic stone into his hand and held it on his palm. He said casually, "Do any of you still have the totem you used to travel here?"

Enlai snapped, "What does this have to do with the Empress?"

Xu said, "I still have mine."

Gideon smiled at the man. Xu's face wrinkled with confusion but he was willing to play Gideon's game.

"Do you remember what I told you about your totem before you travelled here?"

Enlai growled, "You didn't tell us anything, pansy, before we came here. I didn't know who you were. We were told by the elders."

Xu said, "Gideon was the one that found this place. He travelled here first and returned and convinced the elders that travelling to another place was a viable exit plan from our own plane before the comet hit. It was Gideon who wrote the instructions the elders spread among the other dragons."

He turned to Enlai and added, confused, "How did you not know this? The female dragons almost suppressed the knowledge, as they didn't want to leave and were happy to live underground. If it wasn't for Gideon and the other scientists that worked with him we'd be living with no sky."

Xu turned back to Gideon. "I apologise for my brother's ignorance."

Gideon waved it off. "Do you remember what I told you about the totems, how they could take you back if you ever changed your mind?"

Enlai said unhelpfully, "I threw mine away centuries ago. Why do you still have yours? Planning to go back to be the slave of those witches?"

Gideon raised an eyebrow. "You don't know? I go back all the time. About every century. I tell the others left behind how they can travel here. I haven't been in a while, so maybe that's why you haven't heard of new dragons popping up." He waved it off and continued, "I can also send others back with my totem."

Xu hissed. "You sent her back, didn't you?"

Gideon said, "It was clear she wasn't safe here. She was going to be used or maybe even killed. It didn't take much to convince her it was better to be somewhere else."

Enlai asked, "How do we know you're telling the truth? How do we know you haven't killed her or taken her as your mate?"

Gideon pushed the sleeve of his shirt up to show off his brands. "They haven't changed. I'm still mated to my human."

Enlai sneered, "Why would you mate with a human woman?"

Xu ignored Enlai. "The Empress is gone. The Han Empire is no more." His voice showed his relief.

Gideon could tell that for Xu, his fight was over. He just wanted a chance to live the life he wanted to live. It gave Gideon some hope. He had feared the rebels would turn into the monster they feared and force people to their views.

Enlai accused him, "You killed her, didn't you? You just couldn't stand the thought that we would be able to mate with a true dragon instead of a human mongrel."

Enlai drew a sword and charged Gideon. The sudden violence took Gideon by surprise. Before Enlai could finish his assault, the air shimmered and Harlen appeared out of the air in dragon form. He slammed into Enlai, trapping him to the ground under his claw.

Xu, astonished by the sudden appearance of the dragon, stumbled back. Gideon, who had seen the Blazing Blunderbuss in the distance, wasn't as surprised.

He said to his brother, "Good timing."

Xu said, "How is that possible?"

Gideon walked over to Enlai, who swore and struggled to escape from Harlen's claw. "Oh, didn't you know? You are in your own collection, so you can make yourself disappear and appear just like you do items. Harlen and I figured that out centuries ago. It makes me dizzy, so I never do it."

Gideon ducked down by Enlai. "I think we should take this conversation back to the city where we can be a little more civilised."

A rope dropped from the Blazing Blunderbuss, which had caught up with Harlen. Gideon beamed, "Here's my ride. I think you should go with Harlen, Enlai. Enjoy the sights."

Gideon grabbed the rope and pulled himself up. He felt the tug on the rope and looked down to see that Xu followed him. Hara greeted him when he climbed over the edge of the railing, hugging him. Hara wasn't a very demonstrative woman, and they had been arguing, so he held her a little tighter.

She asked, "How's your shoulder?"

He shrugged. "Better now that I'm back with you."

She cupped his cheek. "You're a ridiculous man, Gideon, but you're mine. What's the plan now?"

"We'll discuss the future of Han at the palace. Harlen is going to take Enlai there and make sure he stays put. Now, I wonder why Harlen is here in the first place. I thought he was off enjoying his new wife."

Hara snorted. "I sent for him ages ago. I even managed to get a message to him that you were kidnapped. He knows how to deal with this kind of thing."

"Usually by making it worse. I can do that."

Hara swore softly. "I forgot we should round up that Wukong fellow. He needs to be in any talks about the future of Han." She motioned out to the mountains. "I didn't know dragon fighting could be so brutal. Will they all heal?"

Gideon shrugged. "Most. Some won't be able to fly, though I have heard that my cousin who lost a wing in battle is now able to fly."

Hara asked, surprised by yet another family member, "Cousin?"

Gideon told the tale distractedly. "Yeah. His family run the Middle East, but when he lost his wing in battle his family disowned him. We took him in and called him cousin."

Gideon focused on the present. "Though I doubt it's likely that we're related in any way. My brothers are the only ones I know for a fact who are related to us."

Hara asked, "So he's in your brother's collection?"

Gideon chortled, "Yeah. Though these days he's living in a small town with his wife. I got a letter from him just the other day."

* * *

There was an army at the palace. Smoke rose from one of the towers and more from the palace itself. There wouldn't have been much of the Jade Guard at the palace at all. Even the rebel dragons had left their posts to deal with them.

Wukong stood on the roof of the main palace. It was clear he was waiting for them. Harlen had beaten the guards back and was in the courtyard with Enlai, who was swearing so loudly they could hear him up on the Blazing Blunderbuss.

Gideon slid down the rope to get to the ground. Hara had to agree they didn't have time for entrances. Xu followed Gideon. Hara and a few of her crew also went down. Wukong jumped off the roof and landed in the centre of the courtyard in an impossible leap.

His voice boomed as he said, "We have taken the palace. You are invaders here."

Hara said, "They're refugees. A trifle different, wouldn't you say? It wasn't like they had much choice about coming here."

Gideon said, "Can we at least talk?"

There was a long silence from all of them and Enlai, still pinned by Harlen, screamed, "Never."

Wukong growled, "I'll gut him for you."

Hara put up her hand to stop everyone. "This isn't going anywhere. The Empress is gone and you all have to live with each other. You'll all have a chance to say what you want and we'll see what compromise we can get from there."

Gideon backed her up. "Enlai, you are last. We already know what bile you'll spew over this crowd."

There was a tense silence, as no one knew who would voice their demands first. Xu eventually said, "We want all our people released from the prisons."

Alice coughed. "I already did that. They were wandering around the palace when we escaped. That would have been when you got yourself buried by a wing of the palace."

Xu glanced between Alice and Shilong. He gathered himself. "I would like them brought here to have their story told, for we want the dragon who abused our mates to pay for his crimes."

Gideon added unhelpfully, "The Empress was the one that made it illegal for your kind to take mates."

Xu nodded, but it was Shilong who answered, "She didn't decree for our mates to be tortured until they divorced us. They died centuries ago, and some were horribly mutilated."

There was an awful silence as everyone determinedly did not look at Enlai. He was smart enough to keep quiet. Lala said, "I'll go look for the prisoners. I'm sure Shishi and Angel can help."

Angel twittered her agreement. Harlen hesitated, but let Lala go off on her own. He was Enlai's jailor and they still couldn't trust the man to stand on his own feet without trying escape or fight back.

Alice said, "When they arrive, I wish to say something."

Hara looked to Xu to see if he had anything else to say. He said, "Mostly, we wish to be left alone."

153

Wukong asked, "Do you wish to govern?"

"No, but we do not want to be excluded either. Many of us have held positions in the government and would like to stay. If you treat us as you would others, then we will compromise and pass the reins of the government over to the humans. It's time for the dragons to take a quieter role in society."

He looked at Gideon when he said that. Hara assumed he was thinking of the way the Wyvern Empire operated. Despite the fact that most of the nobility were hybrid dragons, it was still a human empire.

Wukong said, "That would be acceptable. Though dragons would be subject to our laws."

Shilong shifted on his feet before he said, "How can we believe the word of a stranger? If we're to treat together, the time for hiding is over."

Wukong shifted nervously before he made his choice and raised his hands to his head and lifted off the mask. Hara grinned. "Captain Bai. I should have figured that out. I take it you weren't blown off course, then."

"No. We knew you had decided to avoid the Empress's summons, and we needed the winds of change."

Gideon clapped his hands together in pleasure. "I love it when we're known for chaos. It's why I chose her, you know. She changes everything around her, and for the better."

Shilong said, "I saw that from the beginning as well."

Gideon turned to look at Shilong. "Were the orders for just me or my mate as well?"

Xu answered, "Only you, but Shilong's worth is in his ability to gauge a man's heart." Gideon raised an eyebrow as he studied Shilong with a new eye.

Shilong added, "We would never have hurt your mate. So many of ours have been hurt by the Empress and we didn't want to become the monsters we were trying to escape."

Enlai drawled, "How touching."

Gideon asked, "Are you ready to talk?"

Enlai blustered, "If it gets me out from under this brute's claw, then yes, I'll speak."

Harlen blew hot air over Enlai before raising his claw. Enlai stumbled to his feet and dusted himself off. His uniform was no longer crisp and there were frayed cuts from Harlen's sharp claws.

Enlai waved his hand towards Wukong. "Thank you for so easily revealing your identity. It will make it easy to kill you." The threat was clear in his drawled tones.

Hara said, "We won't let you kill him, Enlai."

Enlai looked at Hara. "You're a mongrel human. There is nothing you can do."

Before he could spew more superior drivel over them, Lala returned. She had a single man with her. Alice bowed her head to the man.

Lala said, "The others are resting. They're in bad shape. They only managed to hide in the servants' quarters. This one here speaks Imperial, so he said he would come and talk for the rest of them."

Xu and Shilong recognised him and Xu motioned for him to speak. Before he began, Gideon put up a hand and materialised a coat. He brought it over the man's shoulders. The other dragons looked at Gideon as if he had grown another head.

Hara understood a little about collections. "Gideon doesn't see collections quite the same way as you all do."

The fact that the dragon hadn't materialised his own clothes meant that Enlai and his crew had systematically

155

taken the dragons' collections from them. The new dragon tightened his hands over the edge of the coat. "Thank you. Small kindnesses have been missing from my life. I've come to speak for my fellow men. I was taken eleven years ago. My mate is still alive. I knew that the rebels were close to overthrowing the Empire, so I told her when we were taken not to let them torture her, but to break the bond. She is waiting for me. The others don't have such pleasant stories."

Hara winced, as that wasn't a pleasant story in the least. The dragon waved a hand to indicate Enlai. "The Jade Guard tortured our mates until they divorced us. Some of my kind have been in those holes for over a century. Their mates, even if they did survive the torture, would have died from old age."

Alice coughed. "Do you know about the torture?"

The dragon turned to Alice sharply, then remembered she was the one who had released him. "No," he answered. "We were kept in holes in the ground and to get food we had to pass over our collection."

Hara wondered how many of the dragons had starved because they didn't have enough of a collection. Alice said, "I was told by Enlai about some of the torture."

Enlai scoffed. Harlen slammed his claw next to him and he jumped. Hara said to Alice, "Tell us what Enlai told you."

Alice smoothed a hand over her skirts then started. "Most of it was to intimidate me, so I'll leave out the bits that were just to scare me. He said he mutilated the women if they didn't give in by a certain time. Cutting off limbs."

Xu said, "That's what we know as well. Enlai admitted to this?"

Alice swallowed. "I got the impression he enjoyed it."

Enlai scoffed, "Dirty mongrel. Why would you believe her?"

Shilong stalked up to Enlai. "Did you tell my mate you would mutilate her if she didn't divorce me?"

Enlai shrugged. "It's an intimidation tactic. There was nothing meant by it."

Hara stepped back and Gideon stepped back with her. The others watched the encounter with sick fascination. Shilong was no longer the calm man they had known on the Blazing Blunderbuss.

This was the first time Hara had seen the assassin Gideon had told her about. Hara also realised the others had no idea where this conversation was going, but Gideon did. Was that why she and Gideon were mates? Because they both watched people?

Shilong lifted a hand and turned his palm up. "While you were driving nails through my body you said other things."

Enlai glowered. He must have forgotten what he had said to Shilong when he was torturing him. Hara wanted to know the story of how Alice and Shilong had been taken, but that could wait for when this was all settled.

Shilong continued, "You told me that you had a collection of your own. That you kept it in that place between to preserve it." Enlai's eyes sparked with fear as he remembered the conversation.

Shilong said, "Only someone who is proud of their behaviour collects anything to do with it."

Before the treaty between humans and dragons, dragons were known to collect the heads of humans. Hara knew exactly what Shilong was talking about. When Shilong moved it was lightning fast.

He grabbed Enlai behind his head, pulling him forward and off balance. He spun him around and in the same motion snapped his neck, then dropped him to the ground.

Hara had wondered how dragons were killed when they had such amazing healing abilities. Shilong said to Enlai's body, "You're not welcome in this world."

Gideon said, "I'd have returned him to our original plane like I did the Empress."

Hara glanced at Gideon. She knew he hadn't taken the Empress anywhere but a small fishing village. She didn't mention that now.

Shilong turned to Gideon. "I too know physics, and you could not have done it unless he was in your collection, and he would never have allowed that."

Gideon shrugged, as he didn't disagree with Shilong. The only way they would have been able to convince Enlai to return to his home planet would have been to torture him like he had tortured the emaciated dragon who had born witness just before.

Captain Bai said, "I'll not say his execution wasn't needful. Enlai is already acknowledged by my people to be a criminal."

Shilong said, "It's better if dragons police their own."

He went to Alice, and Hara wondered how she would take Shilong's new facet. Alice reached out her hands to him. Considering Shilong had also been defending her honour, and that Enlai had kidnapped her and threatened to torture her, this was something their relationship could survive.

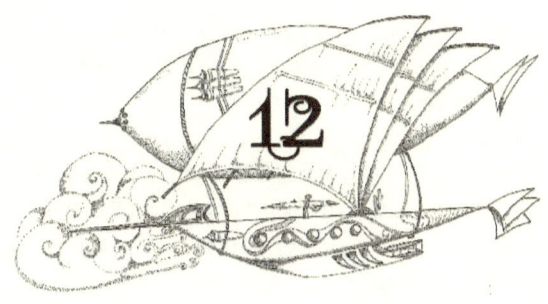

Gideon was on the bridge with Hara. He had his arms around her as they watched the city below. Captain Bai had been rather pleased when they had said they needed to be elsewhere. Notwithstanding they were here because Captain Bai had made sure they were. He wasn't comfortable with the aftermath as much as he had been with the chaos they had been the catalyst for.

Gideon asked, "Have you forgiven me?"

"What for? Getting kidnapped? Getting me kidnapped when I came looking for you?"

"No, for getting you pregnant. You were right, we should've waited for children. I was impatient and I didn't take your feelings into account."

Hara leaned back against him. "Do you really need the words? Surely I've shown that I've forgiven you already. After all, I came after you when you were kidnapped."

"I need the words." His voice was soft as he said it. Hara didn't blame him for needing the words. Maybe more words were what they needed, rather than fewer.

"You're forgiven, but I get to name the child."

Gideon pulled back and spun her around so he could see her face. Hara laughed when she saw his expression.

He was devastated. "I had names picked out already. If it was a boy, he was going to be called Cornelius. I knew this soldier—"

Hara smacked him on his arm. He grinned at her, knowing he was only teasing her. He pulled her back into his arms. He let the silence grow between them but it wasn't uncomfortable. Sometimes the silence said as much as the words.

<hr>

Shilong stood by Alice at the helm. He was watching Hara and Gideon. He asked, "Are they always like that?"

Alice looked at Hara and Gideon standing together in silence, just watching the scenery below them. Alice shook her head. "They're making up after a fight. He didn't tell her that he got her pregnant, and they've been fighting."

Shilong frowned. "I knew of this disagreement, but surely they have finished that argument. That was weeks ago."

Alice chuckled. "Just because I forgave you for not telling me that you had married me doesn't mean that people can't have longer arguments. In fact, you can expect longer arguments between us in the future."

Shilong was shocked. She explained, "I wasn't too mad at you over the marriage thing because I wanted it. I wanted you. Now if you do something I disagree with, it might get very frosty between us."

He nodded solemnly. Alice liked that about him, that he always took her words seriously. She had been around enough of the other Han dragons to know they were not very respectful of female intelligence.

Alice asked, "Are you going to miss Han?"

"It's better that I leave."

"That wasn't what I asked, Shilong. I know why you're here, and wanting to leave Han isn't it. Will you miss it?"

"The dream of Han in my mind is a figment of my imagination. It would die under the harshness of reality." Alice looked at him with kindness in her eyes. Maybe he had seen in Xu and the others that they had different views to himself.

She tried to lighten the conversation by motioning to Shishi, who was curled up sleeping with Angel in a dog bed made for the metal foo-lion. "At least you'll have some company."

Shilong caught one of her hands and brought it up to his lips. He lightly kissed the back of her knuckles. "I have you, and that is enough."

Alice smiled warmly.

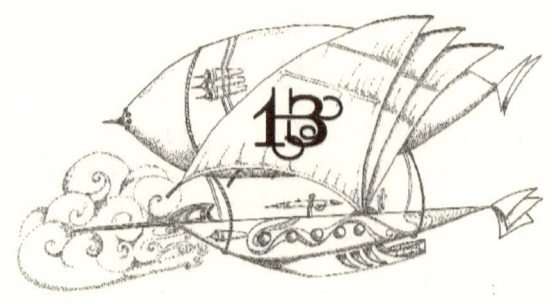

Harlen sharpened his weapons while Lala leaned against the doorway and watched him. He really was a handsome man. His movements were so precise. She liked the idea that he was so dangerous, but she could walk into the room where he was sharpening a plethora of weapons and feel completely safe.

Lala breathed out, her voice gentle. "I love you."

Harlen went still then slowly looked up. Lala blushed when she realised he had not been as absorbed in his task as she had thought.

Lala babbled, "I was going to tell you before, but I—"

He raised an eyebrow. "You wanted to test me?"

"No." She was horrified by the thought and shook her head. "I needed to be sure. You were so sure of me right from the beginning. I knew you were the right man for me in my head, I just had to wait for my heart to catch up."

She closed the distance between them and took up his hands. Moving the weapons aside so she could sit on his lap, she put her arms around his neck. "I've been alone for so long and in places where the best of humanity doesn't shine."

"I'm not human."

"Shush and just listen to me compliment you, Harlen." He raised a single eyebrow but remained quiet.

"Most men treated me like an object or a means to an end, using my dragon hunter abilities. You saw me as a person, and not as something that could be used."

She let out a breath, knowing she was bungling this, and tried again. "Most men saw me as a woman."

"You are a woman," he stated unhelpfully.

Lala knew he was teasing her. "Just as a woman, Harlen. For sex."

This had both his eyebrows lifting. He wasn't a man of many words, but he did manage to get his message across. She sighed. "I was struggling with that idea clashing with reality. You want me to be Lala, and not just a piece of flesh you can feel up."

"I thought you understood that." His brow furrowed.

"I knew that, but I didn't understand it until recently. Forgive me for taking so long."

He gazed at her with his gold eyes and she smiled at him. He pulled her down for a kiss and she tightened her arms around his neck.

＊ ━━━━━━━━━━ ＊

Hara worked on a cot to hang in her room. She wanted to get it finished now, before she became too round to be bothered to do anything.

Harlen and Lala had opted to stay with the Blazing Blunderbuss, as they were heading back to the Empire. It would take longer, but would be a significantly more pleasant trip for Lala. Hara knew how cold it could get travelling on the back of a dragon, even if it was quicker.

Hara looked up at Liam. He was in a corner with Shishi. He was drawing the inner workings of the foo-lion. Hara didn't think it would take long before Liam figured out how to make his own clockwork creatures. Liam had the added advantage of having access to dragons, as the crystals that gave the mechanical creatures their personalities were of dragon design.

Angel sat on Liam's shoulder chittering her own opinion on the whole process. Angel was never far from Shishi, nor Shishi from her. If they had been real creatures Hara would have said they were mated. Unfortunately, neither were designed to have those connections. Hara believed them being together was all they really cared about.

Liam asked, "Did you know that Talen left?"

Hara had found a one-line note from Talen, saying he had gone to find himself. Hara hoped he did find himself. One thing she was sure of was that he wouldn't find himself on the Blazing Blunderbuss. Liam had been privy to some of the awkward conversations she and Talen had, as they had often happened in the engine room where Liam worked as well.

"I suggested to him that he should leave," said Hara. "I just didn't expect him to do it when we still needed him."

Liam shrugged. "I think we did alright without him. That new dragon guy can really fight. I saw him practising with Murphy the other day." Liam paused in his drawing to motion his hands around in a rough approximation of Shilong's fighting style.

Hara asked Liam, "Do you think he'll do right by Alice?"

Liam snorted in humour. "That man is completely head over heels for our first mate. He lets her order him around. I don't know many men that allow that. Except Gideon. Do you think it's a dragon thing?"

Hara shook her head. "No, I think it is a love thing."

Liam shook his head in confusion. "Murphy and Susan are in love, even if they do call themselves friends. They're very well suited to each other, but Susan doesn't order Murphy around."

Hara smiled. "That's because Susan doesn't need to order people around. She figured out how to be herself without having to control everything around her. Alice is like me."

Liam appeared interested, so Hara continued. "We both couldn't control something in our lives, so we've overcompensated. Now we have to control everything. The Blazing Blunderbuss allows us to do that. We're just lucky to have found men who'll let us be in charge."

Liam frowned. "Is that why you freaked over the baby?"

Hara put her hand on her stomach. "It was because he lied about it. He didn't ask me about babies; he just went ahead and did it."

Liam laughed, "I'm sure it was mutual, Hara."

She shook her head with a blush staining her cheeks. "I mean the pregnant part. Dragons can decide that kind of thing. Gideon decided it was a good time to have kids and didn't want to argue with me."

Liam shook his head slowly. "That's different. Doesn't he know we live on a pirate ship?" Hara snorted with laughter, as she knew he was teasing her. Gideon had told her about Enlai's accusations, and that if Shilong hadn't put him down like the mad dog he was, then they might have been chased by other dragons for the suspected murder of a female dragon. There would have been no rest for them then. That had been when Gideon had truly apologised to her and had meant it.

The Empress stared at the wooden tub and wrinkled her nose. She asked the servant, "Why water? I mean, a good sand bath would clean away just as much."

The servant hesitated, but she was getting used to the Empress and what were considered to be her strange ways. Apparently, money could make anything that seemed strange and mad merely eccentric if enough of it was applied.

The servant bowed respectfully. "It's our way, Madam Long."

The Empress narrowed her eyes as the servant reached out a hand to take the clothes from her. This part she didn't mind. She hated wearing clothes. They were so constrictive. If she wanted to move her arms or legs, she had to concentrate so as not to fall on her face. And concentrate she did, because she was tired of being laughed at by humans who were merely children.

The servant helped the Empress to enter the tub, and she sighed. It wasn't too bad. Not nearly as pleasant as sand against scales, but she could live with this.